OLW

The Range Robber

The Range Robber

ALAN IRWIN

A Black Horse Western

ROBERT HALE · LONDON

ISBN 0 7090 6457 8

Robert Hale Limited
Clerkenwell House
Clerkenwell Green
London EC1R 0HT

To June

Photoset in North Wales by
Derek Doyle & Associates, Mold, Flintshire.
Printed and bound in Great Britain by
WBC Book Manufacturers Limited, Bridgend.

ONE

It was around mid-afternoon when Jack Silver rode into the small town of Bridger, located in a valley south of the Texas Panhandle. He was on his way from South Texas to Colorado, where his parents ran a small ranch near Pueblo.

Jack had served as a sheriff in South Texas for the past three years, but when the time came round for elections again he had decided not to stand, despite pleas from many quarters for him to do so. He had proved to be a respected and conscientious law officer, highly proficient in the use of both the Colt .45 Peacemaker which he carried on his right hip and his Winchester .44 rifle.

He had felt a growing restlessness for the past six months, with a hankering to visit his parents in Colorado and stay with them a while, in the shadow of the towering Rocky Mountain Range.

Riding along the one and only street of Bridger, Jack spotted a livery stable on his right. He headed for it, stopped outside, and dismounted. The owner, Jake Durrell, was standing in the entrance.

'Howdy,' said Jack. 'I figure on staying here overnight. Can you take my horse?'

'Howdy,' replied Durrell, admiring the animal, a big, handsome, chestnut gelding, with a white star and stripe on its head. 'Sure I can. I'll take him in and feed and water him right now.'

He regarded the stranger with interest. The man in front of him was in his early thirties, well-built, clean-shaven and a little over average height. He was wearing a black Texas hat and dust-stained clothing of good quality. A Colt .45 Peacemaker rested in a holster on his right hip.

There was, thought Durrell, as he took the reins of the chestnut, an air of quiet self-assurance about the stranger, as if he were, or had been, someone in authority.

'Two things I want, more than anything else,' said Jack, smiling. 'First of all, I need a bath. Then, right after that, I'd like a good meal. Maybe you could point me in the right direction.'

'That's easy,' said Durrell, gesturing down the street. 'You see the barber's shop along there? That's where you can get a bath. As for the meal, the only restaurant we have here is right opposite, on the other side of the street. It's run by a widow, Mrs Harris. I can vouch for the quality of the food she serves up.'

Jack thanked Durrell and walked along to the barber's shop. Half an hour later, feeling a lot cleaner and with most of the dust shaken out of his clothes, he walked back along the street and crossed over to the restaurant.

A middle-aged woman, who was just about to leave the dining-room for the kitchen at the rear, turned as Jack came in.

'I'll be with you in a few minutes,' she said, then turned and left the room.

The only other customer in the dining-room was a young woman seated at one of the tables. As Jack glanced at her, she looked towards him, and he was struck by her beauty. She was slim in build, with a tanned, oval face framed by shoulder-length auburn hair, and, thought Jack, probably in her mid-twenties. She was dressed in riding clothes.

Jack sat down a couple of tables away from the woman and shortly afterwards Mrs Harris came in, took their orders, and served them a few minutes later.

Jack enjoyed the meal, and was just having a drink of coffee prior to leaving when he saw a man pass outside the window facing on to the street. A moment later, the same man entered the dining-room and stood just inside the door, looking around.

He was a bearded man, of average height, heavily built, with hard eyes and a surly expression on his face. He wore a right-hand gun. As the man swayed slightly on his feet, Jack got the impression that he had been drinking. The man looked at Jack, then at the young woman, who recognized him as Bart Sinclair, elder son of Jed Sinclair, owner of the big Box S Ranch which straddled most of the valley.

Sinclair walked across and sat down at the young woman's table. Startled, she looked across at him. He scowled at her. She could smell the whisky on his breath.

'You still around, Mary Carson?' he said. 'When my pa told you folks to quit your ranch, he meant it. You've got one more day to leave. If you stay on after that, you're in real trouble. Pa's set on getting hold of that land you're sitting on, and he made you a good offer to hand it over. We need it for the Box S.'

Jack had overheard what the man was saying, and he listened to the young woman's reply.

'That land is ours,' she said, 'and a lot of hard work has gone into setting our ranch up. You ain't got no right to try and force us off it. We're not leaving. Mother, father and myself, we're all agreed on that.'

'You Carsons are all fools,' said Sinclair, menacingly. 'Stay here and you're going to get pa all riled up. There's no knowing what he'll do to you.'

'You're just a pair of greedy bullies,' said Mary, heatedly. 'I don't want to speak to you any more.'

She got up and walked over to the table next to Jack's and sat down again. Sinclair followed her, and sat down opposite her once again. His face was red with rage. She shrank back in her chair as he leaned over towards her.

'You heard what the lady said,' Jack intervened. 'She don't want your company.'

Sinclair glared across at him. 'Keep out of this,' he said, harshly. 'I'm Bart Sinclair. My father owns the Box S Ranch in the valley.'

'That don't mean nothing to me,' said Jack. 'Am I

supposed to be scared? If you don't leave the lady alone I'm going to have to give you a lesson in manners.'

Just then, Mrs Harris came into the dining-room. Looking towards her three customers, she sensed the tension in the air, halted, and stood watching the two men.

As Sinclair rose from the table, Jack did likewise and stood facing him. Sinclair, proficient both as a rough and tumble fighter and in the handling of a six-gun, thought first of gunning the interfering stranger down, but something about the look of calm self-assurance on Jack's face irritated him, and he decided he'd like to get his hands on the man standing in front of him.

Jack, poised on the balls of his feet, awaited Sinclair's rush. When it came he side-stepped quickly and smoothly out of his opponent's path. Then, as Sinclair blundered past him, arms flailing, Jack lifted the gun from his opponent's holster and stuck out a leg, which tripped Sinclair and sent him sprawling on the floor. Jack threw the gun into the far corner of the room.

Enraged, Sinclair got up, turned to face Jack, and reached for his six-gun. Finding the holster empty he paused for a moment, cursing, then launched himself at Jack once more. This time his opponent stood his ground, but as Sinclair reached him Jack dodged his blows, grasped Sinclair's vest with his two hands, and sank down to roll over backwards, pulling his opponent with him. As Sinclair fell forward over him, Jack placed his foot against his opponent's stomach and pushed with all his strength. Sinclair, projected through the air, fell on one of the tables which collapsed under him. His head collided with the floor, and he lay still.

Jack looked over at Mrs Harris, who was staring at the man lying flat on his back on the floor.

'I'm mighty sorry for the damage to that table, ma'am,' he said. 'I'll get it fixed for you. Meantime, we don't want the man doing any more damage in here. You got something I can use to tie him up?'

She hesitated, then hurried out of the room and came back almost immediately with a length of stout cord. Jack knelt down beside Sinclair and deftly bound his wrists together, then his ankles. He rose and walked over to pick up Sinclair's six-gun, which he tucked inside his own belt. Then he spoke to Mary.

'He's just knocked out temporary, I reckon,' he said. 'I couldn't help hearing about the fix you and your folks are in. This Box S Ranch is a big spread?'

'It's big,' she replied. 'Much too big for us, if it comes to a fight.'

Just then, the figure on the floor stirred, and all three of them looked down at Sinclair. His eyes opened and he shook his head, then stared in disbelief at the three faces above him and at his tied hands and feet.

He opened his mouth and from it came a stream of foul profanity. Jack shook his head, tut-tutted, bent over the man on the floor, and wrenched the bandanna from around his neck. Then he turned Sinclair over so that he was lying face-down, planted one knee on his back, forced the bandanna into his open mouth, and secured it as tightly as he could at the back of Sinclair's neck. The flow of profanity was arrested. Jack turned to the two women.

'I'm sorry about that, ladies,' he said, leading them to the other side of the room, so that Sinclair could not overhear what they were saying. 'This man just don't seem to have no manners at all. He just ain't been brung up right.'

'What are you going to do with him?' asked Mary, who had watched Sinclair's downfall with considerable satisfaction.

'Send him on his way back to the Box S, I guess,' said Jack. 'D'you reckon there are any other Box S men in town just now?'

'No,' said Mrs Harris. 'Not at this time of day. This one usually comes in alone. Visits the saloon quite a lot.'

'Right,' said Jack. 'We'll send him on his way, then.'

He walked over to Sinclair and removed the cord from his ankles, but not from his wrists. Then he ordered him to walk outside and mount his horse. Two people about to enter the restaurant, and several people out in the street, gaped as they saw the elder son of the owner of the Box S, shaking with fury, gagged, with wrists bound, climb into the saddle.

'You can go now, Sinclair,' said Jack. 'And tell that

father of yours that what he's doing is against the law, and that I'm aiming to hang around here and take a hand if he don't mend his ways.'

He slapped Sinclair's horse on the flank and it trotted out of town, up the valley, in the direction of the Box S ranch house.

'D'you mean what you just said?' asked Mary Carson as they watched Sinclair leave.

'Sure,' replied Jack. 'The big ranchers like Sinclair's father have got to be made to see that they can't ride roughshod over small ranchers and home-steaders. I take it there's no law officer around here?'

'The nearest lawman is well over a hundred miles from here,' she replied. 'As for you staying around here, I reckon you'd be wise to ride on right now, before Jed Sinclair sends his men after you. But before you go, I'd like to thank you for butting in when you did. It sure did pleasure me to see the look on Bart Sinclair's face when you sent him flying through the air like that.'

'I don't aim to leave,' said Jack, 'and the first thing I have to do is to get you safely back to your folks. The way Bart Sinclair was acting, you ain't safe riding the range alone.'

'All right,' said Mary, a little shaken by the events of the last half hour, and not averse to spending more time in Jack's company. 'I'd be obliged. I'm ready to leave now.'

They left as soon as Jack had collected his horse from the livery stable, and as they rode out of town he told her his name and about his intention to visit his parents in Colorado. Then he asked her about the trouble between her family and the Box S.

She told him that her father, John Carson, was the first rancher to start raising cattle in the valley. He had bought a stretch of land along the river three years ago, four miles down the valley from Bridger's present location, and had hired two hands to help him look after a small herd of longhorns driven up from Texas – all he could afford to buy at the time. His intention was, when firmly established, to use any profits to purchase more land and expand his operation.

Then, just a year ago, Jed Sinclair had bought a long stretch of land along the river and had driven a big herd into the valley. He located his ranch buildings ten miles up the valley from the Carson ranch, and the small town of Bridger sprang into being. In the subsequent twelve months he had brought more cattle in and his cows were now spread over the whole of the valley, causing some annoyance to Carson when strays came on to his land.

Apart from this, Sinclair had not bothered the Carsons at first, but a month ago he had approached Mary's father with an offer to buy him out. It was clear that he wanted the whole of the valley for his own cattle. When Carson refused the offer, Sinclair raised it, then turned ugly and threatened to evict Carson by force when the rancher said he wasn't interested in moving, not at any price. Since then, Carson and Sinclair had not met again, but several times a large group of Box S riders had passed close to the Carson ranch buildings, making threatening gestures and shouting insults.

14   *The Range Robber*

times a large group of Box S riders had passed close
to the Carson ranch buildings, making threatening
gestures and shouting insults.

TWO

The sun was setting behind the high ground at the
head of the valley as Jack and Mary approached the
Carson ranch. A man was standing just outside the
ranch house looking in their direction. He was a tall
man, slim in build, and bearded.

'There's Father,' said Mary.

Carson looked closely at Mary's companion as the
couple rode up to him and dismounted. Carson's
wife, Ellen, came out of the house and stood by her
husband. She was a handsome woman, slim, her hair
still unflecked by grey. It was easy to see where Mary's
good looks came from. Mary introduced Jack, then
told her parents what had happened in Bridger.

'Damn Sinclair!' said Carson angrily. 'He ain't
got no right to threaten us like this.' He turned to
Jack. 'We sure are obliged to you, Mr Silver, for
helping Mary out like that. But I'm afraid the
Sinclairs ain't going to take too kindly to what you
did to Bart. I reckon your best plan would be to ride
out of the valley just as soon as you can. Sinclair has
ten hands in his outfit, as well as his sons, Bart and

15

Clem, and some of them look like gunslingers to me.'

'I just can't do that,' said Jack. 'There's a stubborn streak in me that's caused me a lot of trouble in the past. It seems to take over when I meet up with people like the Sinclairs. If you'd like me to, I figure to stay around here and help you if Sinclair tries to force you out and take your ranch over. I've just finished a three-year spell as a sheriff in South Texas, so I've had some dealings with people like the Sinclairs, who reckon they're above the law. I can't leave here knowing the danger you're all in.'

'We sure could do with some help,' said Carson. 'My two hands ain't exactly fighting men, and neither am I, for that matter. But even with you here, what can we do to stop Sinclair and his men when he decides to move in and throw us off the ranch?'

'My guess,' said Jack, 'is that Sinclair's first priority, after what happened to Bart, will be to deal with me. The whole town knows by now how his son was outfought, and tied up and gagged by me. Sinclair has lost face and he knows it. And I could see from the look on Bart's face that he was real hopping mad himself.

'I've met Bart, of course,' Jack went on, 'but what are Jed Sinclair and his other son like?'

'The father,' replied Carson, 'is a big bully of a man, mean-natured, about six feet tall and over-weight. His son Clem is a smaller version of his father. It was a bad day for us when they rode into the valley.'

'What can we do to help ourselves?' asked Mary.

'Get ready for a visit from Bart Sinclair and some of the Box S hands,' replied Jack. 'They'll have heard in town that I rode off towards your ranch with you, and Sinclair'll be mighty keen to get his hands on me. I figure that maybe they'll come tonight, but probably not for another two or three hours.

'I'm sorry to bring this on you,' he went on. 'I could go away and hide somewhere, but if they come and don't find me here, I think they're liable to do you harm. Are you willing for me to stay here and help you?'

'We're more than willing,' replied Carson. 'We're darned grateful. We could see that a showdown with Sinclair was coming any time.'

'Could you get the two hands in here?' asked Jack. 'I think we should organize a reception committee for our visitors.'

'Sure,' said Carson, and asked Mary to go to the small shack which served as a bunkhouse and fetch them.

When she returned with the two men, Hank Randle and Josh Ranger, Carson introduced them to Jack. They were both men in their middle fifties, experienced cowhands, and the exact opposite in build. Randle was short and stocky, Ranger tall and slim. Carson told them about Mary's encounter with Bart Sinclair earlier in the day, and about Jack's expectation of a visit by Bart Sinclair and Box S hands during the night.

'I wouldn't blame you men,' he said, 'if you

figured you didn't want any part in this fight.'

'You know we ain't gunfighters,' said Randle. 'In fact, we've only got one old Colt .45 between us. But I ain't quitting – and I figure Josh feels the same way as I do.'

Ranger nodded emphatically. 'What's the plan of action?' he asked.

'I'm taking Mr Silver's advice on that,' Carson replied. 'He was a lawman in South Texas for three years.'

'As soon as we can,' said Jack, 'we'll all move into the barn and leave a light burning inside the house. We'll take some food and drink and everything else we need for the night. And we'll take all the firearms and ammunition we can lay our hands on. I have a Colt .45 Peacemaker myself, and a rifle. How about you, Mr Carson?'

'A Winchester rifle is all,' replied the rancher, 'but with plenty of ammunition.'

'That's two rifles and two six-guns, then,' said Jack. 'Enough for us to put up a good fight. I'll use my six-gun. One of you can have my rifle.'

While Mary and her mother got the things ready to take into the barn, Jack and the others walked over to it, carrying an oil lamp, and went inside. It was a tall structure, with a loft which could be reached by a ladder. There was an opening in the wall of the loft through which the front wall of the house could be observed. The two buildings were about thirteen yards apart.

Jack climbed up to the loft and inspected the wall

facing the house. Then he climbed down and looked at the wide timber door of the barn.

'This is what we'll do,' he said. 'We'll all climb up into the loft and then I'll pull the ladder up. We'll leave the barn door wide open so's they won't suspect there's anybody inside. With the light showing in the house they'll figure we're all in there. We'll use the opening in the loft wall for firing one rifle through and we'll knock a bit of boarding out of the wall so that the other rifle and the six-guns can fire towards the house as well.'

Randle found a heavy hammer and handed it to Jack, who climbed into the loft and knocked out a horizontal piece of boarding at eye level. Then they all assisted in carrying the things from the house up into the loft. When they had all assembled there, Jack pulled up the ladder and laid it on the floor, against a wall.

Jack extinguished the lamp, then they all settled down in the darkness, sitting on small piles of hay, except for Jack and Randle, who were watching out for any sign of intruders outside. They all partook of the food and drink they had brought with them.

It was a clear night, with a half moon showing. By its light, Jack could clearly see the front wall and door of the house. The night air was still and there was no sign of any intruders until well after midnight, when they heard a slight sound which appeared to come from near the barn door. Jack whispered to Carson and Ranger to take up positions next to himself and Randle, ready to fire on anyone outside. Then he whispered to his companions to stay quiet.

Listening intently, they heard the sound of muted voices down below, and saw the light from a match which flared up for a brief instant. Then they saw the dim but steady light from an oil lamp, which Carson now remembered had been hanging from a peg on the wall near the barn door. The subdued conversation below continued for a short time, then the lamp was extinguished and there was silence.

Moments later, the four men in the loft saw the shadowy figures of four men stealthily approaching the house. The light was still showing from inside.

'Let them have it,' said Jack.

The hail of fire from above and behind them brought one of the intruders to the ground, where he lay, writhing, and holding his leg. Two more were hit low down, but not sufficiently badly to prevent them from twisting round, returning the fire, and hopping and running, as fast as their wounded legs would take them, out of sight behind the barn.

The fourth man, who appeared to be unhit, turned quickly and ran to the barn door, returning the fire as he did so, until he disappeared from view. The four men in the barn stopped firing and listened in silence until, suddenly, a match was struck down below, and a moment later a man carrying a lighted oil lamp ran towards the centre of the floor of the barn, firing towards the loft as he did so. One of the bullets sang past Jack's ear and he shrank back momentarily. Reaching the centre of the floor, the man below stopped abruptly, fired two more shots upwards, then hurled the lamp up into the loft. As the lamp left his hand, his head and neck were visible from Jack's position on the floor of the loft, and a bullet from Jack's Peacemaker drilled into his forehead.

The lamp fell on to the small pile of hay against which Mary was crouching. The oil spilled out and ignited and in a moment the bottom of Mary's long skirt was alight. Jack grabbed a blanket, pulled Mary away from the burning hay, and wrapped the blanket tightly around her skirt and legs. Meanwhile, the others pushed the small quantity of burning hay from the loft on to the bare earth floor of the barn, where the flames could do no harm, and would soon die out.

As Jack unwrapped the blanket from Mary, and checked that the flames on her skirt had all been extinguished, her mother came over and knelt beside her.

'It's all right, Mother,' said Mary, her voice shaking a little. 'All I can feel is one small burn on the ankle.'

Jack called to Randle, who was watching the house through the opening in the wall.

'Is that wounded man still out there?' he asked.

'Yes,' replied Randle. 'He's holding his leg. I guess he's too scared to move in case we shoot him.'

They waited until the flames on the floor of the barn had died away. Then Jack put the ladder in position, and, with his six-gun in his hand, he climbed down to the floor and walked over to the door. He stood there for a while, listening, but the only sound he could hear was an occasional groan from the man lying on the ground outside.

He left the barn and walked around the house and all the outbuildings. Behind the barn, tied to a rail of the small corral, he found two Box S horses. He was now convinced that the two wounded men who had moved behind the stable after the shooting had ridden off.

He returned to the barn and told the others to light the lamp and come down. When they had all done this, Jack took the lamp and held it over the man on the floor. It was Bart Sinclair. Jack turned to Mary and her mother, who were staring down at the dead body.

'You can go into the house now, I reckon,' he said. 'I can't see Sinclair bothering us any more tonight.'

As the two women walked across to the house, the four men went over to the man lying on the ground outside. Jack picked up the man's six-gun, lying several yards away from its owner, then, carrying the lamp, he walked on and looked into the man's face.

'That's Lassiter,' said Carson, 'one of Sinclair's hands.'

Lassiter was holding his leg just above the knee, and there was a small pool of blood on the ground underneath it. He looked up at them, his face twisted with pain and apprehension.

'Better take him into the house,' said Carson.

Randle and Ranger lifted the wounded man, carried him into the house, and laid him down on an old blanket on the floor of the living-room. Jack knelt down by him, slit the leg of his pants upwards from the bottom, and had a good look at the wound. Ellen Carson peered at it over his shoulder.

'I don't reckon the bullet's still in there,' said Jack, 'but it sure made a bit of a mess before it passed on.'

'I think you're right,' said Ellen Carson. 'I'll get some warm water and a bandage.'

When she came back she knelt down on the floor and attended to the wound. When she had finished, Jack helped Lassiter up and sat him on a chair. The Box S man had not spoken since they brought him inside.

'Maybe you're wondering, Lassiter,' said Jack, 'why we're bothering to help a villain like yourself. The reason is that we've got a job for you to do. Sinclair's lying in the barn with a bullet through his head. I shot him when he tried to set fire to the barn. The other two men who came with you have ridden off. We're going to sling Sinclair over the back of his horse and you can take him back to the Box S.'

Ranger went for the two Box S horses and when he returned Jack and the two hands lashed the body of Bart Sinclair over the back of one of them and helped Lassiter to climb into the saddle of the other. Then they watched silently, with Carson, as Lassiter rode slowly off into the darkness, leading the horse that was carrying Sinclair's body.

THREE

After Carson had led the way back into the house,
they all sat down to discuss the situation.

'Well,' said Carson, 'there's no knowing what
Sinclair'll do when Lassiter rides in with Bart's body.'

'He'll come here with all his men,' said Jack, 'after
daylight probably, and he'll be out for revenge.
There'll be too many of them for us to fight off.
That's why I reckon you should all go into Bridger
pronto, before the Box S men get here. Have you any
friends in town you could stay with?'

'I have a cousin in Bridger,' replied Carson. 'He
and his wife run the store. We're pretty close, and
I'm sure us three can stay with them for a while.'

'Hank and me can bunk down in the livery stable,'
said Ranger. 'Jake Durrell's a good friend of ours.'

'But what about you?' Carson asked Jack. 'What
d'you figure on doing?'

'I'm going into hiding,' replied Jack. 'Lassiter will
tell Sinclair that I was the one who killed his son, and
I'll be the one he's after. I'm pretty sure the rest of

24

you'll be safe in town. I don't think even Sinclair would dare to harm you there.

'I'm pretty sure,' he went on, 'that Sinclair'll be concentrating on tracking me down, so I figure you men should be able to ride out to the ranch now and then to keep an eye on things. But I don't think it would be a good idea for anybody to stay overnight there.'

At Jack's request, Carson told him just where the Box S ranch buildings were located. He asked Jack where he was intending to hide.

'Don't know yet,' said Jack. 'Maybe you can help. What I need is a hiding-place for me and my horse from which there's a good view of Sinclair's ranch buildings. Anybody got any ideas?'

Ranger, who had been longer in the area than any of the others, spoke up.

'I know just the place,' he said. 'Right on top of the ridge that borders the valley on the south, there's a wide, deepish hollow where you and your horse could hide. This hollow's located right opposite the Box S buildings, and I reckon that anybody up there with a good pair of field-glasses should be able to keep a close watch on what's going on down below. There's a gully running from the hollow down the south side of the ridge.'

'Thanks,' said Jack. 'That sounds exactly like the place I'm looking for.'

'I've got some field-glasses you can take with you,' said Carson, and went away to find them. When he returned with the glasses, he spoke to Jack.

'I'm wondering,' he said, 'what'll happen if the Box S men ride out to our ranch and find us all gone. D'you think they'll set fire to the buildings?'

'I doubt it,' said Jack. 'Don't forget that Sinclair's figuring to take those buildings over. And in any case, I don't think he'll bother you so long as I'm on the loose. I aim to keep him and his men occupied for a while.'

They all left the ranch an hour later. Jack was carrying a bedroll and some provisions which Mary had put together for him. When they reached the outskirts of town Jack left the others, telling them he would ride in at night-time if he wanted to contact them for any reason.

'If you want to do that,' Carson told him, 'knock on the door at the back of the store.'

'I'll do that,' said Jack, then headed west up the valley, through the darkness, until he judged that he was fairly close to the Box S ranch house. Then he swung south and was soon climbing the slope of the ridge which bordered the valley.

When he reached the top of the ridge, he started to look for the hollow Ranger had described. It took him only ten minutes, riding slowly westward along the ridge, to reach it. He rode down into it, dismounted, and tethered his horse. Then he waited for sun-up.

When it came, he lay down at the lip of the hollow and kept the Box S ranch buildings under observation. There was already some activity down below. At the top of a small rise behind the house two men were digging a hole in the ground. Not long after they had finished, two men came out of the ranch house, followed by four others carrying a large bundle. They were joined by six more men who came from the bunkhouse, and the whole party climbed to the top of the rise.

As Jack watched the bundle being lowered into the hole he was sure that he was watching the burial of Bart Sinclair. When the brief ceremony was over and the hole had been filled in, ten men, including the two who had first come out of the ranch house, mounted their horses and rode off fast down the valley towards Bridger. Jack guessed that they were heading for the Carson ranch.

He stayed where he was all day, allowing his horse to graze in the hollow. From time to time he saw two men moving around the Box S buildings, one of them limping slightly. Then, just before nightfall, he saw a bunch of riders, nine in all, arrive back at the ranch house. He wondered what had happened to the tenth rider who had left with the others in the morning.

He stayed where he was for the next three hours, then saddled up and rode down the slope into the valley. He headed for Bridger, keeping off the main trail between the Box S and town. When he arrived there he left his horse tethered in a small thicket just outside town and proceeded cautiously on foot, avoiding the main street by moving along the rear of the buildings.

He was still some way from the back of the store

when he saw ahead of him the flare of a match and a man's face, briefly illuminated as he lit a cigarette. The man, standing close to the rear of the building next to the store, had his back to Jack. After looking in the man's direction for the next five minutes, during which he made no move, Jack decided that probably he had been left behind by Sinclair to keep a watch on the store in case Jack came there to see the Carsons.

He went back to his horse for some rope, then, keeping close to the backs of the intervening buildings, he slowly advanced on the watching man until, finally, he was able to run up softly behind him and rap him over the head with the barrel of his Peacemaker.

The man, who was short and slim, collapsed on the ground, unconscious, and before he came round Jack disarmed him and trussed him up so effectively that he was barely capable of moving. Using his own bandanna, together with the one he took off his victim, he gagged and blindfolded the man. Then, leaving him on the ground, he went to search for his horse and found it at a nearby hitching rail on the street. It was a pinto, bearing the Box S brand.

Jack led the horse to the man lying on the ground, hoisted him up across the horse's back, then led the animal back to the thicket in which his own horse was standing. He tied the pinto to a tree, pulled the bound man off his horse, checked the rope around him and left him lying on the ground. Then he walked along to the store, keeping out of sight as before, and knocked on the back door. It was opened by the storekeeper's wife, Emily Drury.

'I'm Jack Silver,' said Jack. 'The Carsons are here?'

She nodded and beckoned him inside, quickly closing the door behind him.

'They thought that maybe you'd be looking in,' she said. 'I'm Emily Drury.'

She led him through to the living-room, where the Carsons and her husband were seated.

'We have a visitor,' she said, and introduced Jack to her husband, George Drury, then motioned him to sit down. Jack spoke to Carson.

'Has Sinclair bothered you at all today?' he asked.

'I think we're safe in town,' said Carson, 'but Sinclair's men have been to the ranch looking for you and they've searched every building in town as well. Jed and Clem Sinclair were both riding with their men. Jed Sinclair came in here looking like a crazy man. He said that they were going after you and that there was no way you could get away. He told us that as soon as they'd caught up with you they'd come to take over our ranch and if we didn't move out peaceable-like we'd be in real trouble.'

'Are the two hands all right?' asked Jack.

'Yes,' replied Carson. 'Sinclair hasn't bothered them. I reckon,' he went on,' that you'd better take care when you come to see us here. Sinclair might get the idea that you're likely to do that, and post a man in town to watch out for you.'

'He already did that,' said Jack, 'but I spotted him in time. I've got him tied up in a thicket just outside town. I'm going to take him back with me and leave him tied on his horse not far from the Box S ranch house. It'll be another surprise for Sinclair when the man's found.'

He described the man and his horse as best he could and asked Carson and the storekeeper if they knew who he was.

'That's Purvis,' said Drury. 'He comes in here sometimes. He's a mean-looking man. I heard that he had a reputation as a gunslinger.'

'What are you going to do after you leave Purvis?' asked Mary. There was a worried look on her face.

'I'm going to the place I went to last night,' replied Jack. 'I'll stay there as long as I can. Looking down on the ranch like that I get a rough idea of what Sinclair's up to. If I see any riders coming towards me I'll ride down the south side of the ridge and find me a new hiding-place until I can go back to the hollow again later.

'What I'm aiming to do for the time being,' he went on, 'is to keep Sinclair occupied in trying to track me down. That way, you'll be safe. But while he's doing that I've got to think up some way of stopping him from ever bothering you again in the future.

'What I'm going to do,' he continued, 'is to get hold of two good friends of mine, Tex Foster and Milt Grayson, and ask them to come and help me out. They were my deputies when I was serving as a sheriff in South Texas. They quit not long before I did. Tex's folks run a store in Santa Fe and he told me he was going to visit with them for a while. Milt was going to stay with a brother of his who runs a livery stable in Albuquerque. What's the best way I can get a message to them?'

'There's a way-station on the stagecoach route that passes twelve miles east of here,' said Carson. 'You write your messages down and I'll get Ranger to take them there tomorrow. He'll see that they're passed on to the stagecoach driver to hand in at the first telegraph office he comes to.'

Drury, the storekeeper, brought paper and a pen, and Jack sat down at the table to write the messages. When he had finished, he put them in an envelope which he handed to Carson. He told them he had asked Tex and Milt to hightail it to Bridger and contact Mr Drury at the store, without revealing their identities to anyone else.

'Maybe,' he said, 'it would be as well not to tell Ranger what's in the messages. The fewer the people who know about it, the better.'

At Mrs Drury's insistence, Jack had a quick meal before leaving. He told them he would contact them again as soon as he could. Mary accompanied him to the door.

'When will that be?' she asked.

'I just can't say,' he replied. 'It all depends on Sinclair.'

'Just take care,' she said.

'That I aim to do,' he assured her.

He walked back to the thicket, hoisted the wriggling Purvis across the back of the pinto and lashed

him on. He mounted his own horse and led the
pinto up the valley towards the Box S ranch house.
He left it a quarter of a mile from the house, turned,
and rode back down the valley for a short distance.
Then he turned, and headed for the ridge where he
had spent the previous day. Reaching the hollow on
top of the ridge, he tethered his horse and slept until
dawn, when he renewed his surveillance of the Box S
buildings in the valley below.

As he swept the area with his field-glasses, a horse
standing by the pasture fence caught his eye. It was
the pinto that he had released a few hours earlier.
And the bound figure of Purvis was still lying across
its back.

It was half an hour before Purvis was spotted by a
hand who glanced across at the pasture as he was
walking from the bunkhouse to the cookshack. The
hand ran over to the pinto, shouting to another
hand to go and bring Sinclair.

By the time Jed Sinclair came out of the house,
hands had taken Purvis down from his horse, had
removed the gag and blindfold and were untying the
rope around his body. When they had done this,
Purvis, almost incoherent with rage, was unable to
stand for a while until the circulation in his legs was
restored. When he had calmed down a little, he told
the Sinclairs what had happened.

'You any idea who did this?' the rancher asked
him.

'No,' replied Purvis. 'I didn't see anybody before I
was hit, and I was blindfolded before I came round.'

'It ain't hard to guess who it was,' said the rancher. 'It must have been Silver, on his way to see the Carsons. I'm surprised you didn't spot him before he got you.'

Purvis flushed. 'It was dark,' he said, 'and he snuck up on me from behind.'

'How long is it since he left you?' asked Sinclair.

'It seemed a whole lot longer,' replied Purvis, angrily, 'but I reckon it was maybe four or five hours ago.'

'He's well away by now, then,' said the rancher, turning to his son.

'Silver's hiding out somewhere,' he said. 'He's got to be found. We'll take ten hands with us. We'll all ride to Bridger and search the town again. Then, if he ain't there, I'll take five men and search the Carson ranch and the eastern section of the valley, while you take five men and search the western section. And remember, from that information we picked up yesterday in town, Silver's riding a big chestnut with a white star and stripe. If we don't find Silver today, we'll search the ridges and the ground just outside the valley tomorrow.'

Half an hour later, watching from the ridge, Jack saw twelve riders, who had assembled outside the Box S ranch house, move off in the direction of Bridger.

FOUR

In the afternoon of the same day on which Purvis had been found, bound to his horse on the Box S ranch, Carson's hand Josh Ranger left town, bound for the stagecoach line way-station. He was carrying Jack's messages to his friends. When he arrived there, he waited until the stage pulled in and handed the envelope to the driver. Then he headed back towards Bridger.

Riding up the valley, a few miles east of the Carson ranch, he was skirting a group of trees in his path, when six mounted men suddenly rode out and surrounded him. As he came to a halt, he recognized them as Jed Sinclair of the Box S and five of his hands. He looked into the menacing face of the rancher.

'It's a stroke of luck for us, Ranger,' said Sinclair, 'finding you out here like this. We're looking for Silver, and I've got an idea that maybe you can tell us where he's hiding.'

'I don't know where he is,' said Ranger, his eyes shifting from Sinclair's face. 'Ain't seen him for two days.'

'I think you're lying,' said the rancher. 'It'll be dark soon. You'll come back with us to the Box S, and maybe we can jog your memory.'

By the time they reached the Box S darkness had fallen. Ranger was put into a small shed near the cookshack and was tied hand and foot. The door of the shack was bolted on the outside. Sinclair and his men went for a meal, and while they were eating this, Clem Sinclair and the other five hands rode in and joined them.

Soon after the meal was over two of the hands, Purvis and Cameron, took Ranger into the barn with his hands still bound. They stood him with his back against one of the posts supporting the loft and bound him tightly to it. Soon after, the two Sinclairs walked in and stood looking at Ranger for a short while. Then Jed Sinclair spoke.

'I'm pretty sure, Ranger,' he said, 'that you know where we can find Silver. Are you going to tell us now, or do we have to think up some way of making you talk?'

Ranger licked his lips. 'I don't know where he is,' he said.

Cameron, a big man with a vicious look about him, spoke to the rancher.

'Let me beat it out of him, Mr Sinclair,' he said. 'It shouldn't take long.'

'No, Cameron,' said Sinclair. 'I've thought of a way to make him talk without beating him almost sense-less first.'

He spoke to Purvis, who left the barn and

returned a few minutes later carrying a branding iron and a bundle of firewood. He cleared a space on the ground, and using the firewood he started a small fire, then placed the end of the branding iron in the flames.

Fascinated, Ranger stared down at the iron as it heated up on the fire. Sinclair walked up to him and undid the top buttons of the prisoner's shirt, revealing the flesh beneath. In desperation, Ranger struggled violently, without success, to free himself from the rope binding him to the post.

The rancher waited until the iron was well heated, then bent down to pick it up, and for a moment he held it with the end close to his face.

'Just about right,' he said, and walked up to the prisoner.

'Let me know, Ranger,' he said, 'when you're ready to tell us what we want to know.'

Deliberately, he raised the branding iron and as the prisoner cringed in apprehension, he briefly touched the hot end against the flesh at the top of Ranger's chest.

Ranger screamed, and the air was tainted with the smell of burning flesh. Sinclair replaced the branding iron on the fire for a short while, then picked it up again, raised it, and approached the prisoner.

'No, no!' shouted Ranger. 'I'll tell you.'

Sinclair held the hot end of the iron a few inches from the prisoner's chest. 'I'm listening,' he said, 'and if I find out that you've been lying, you'll get more of the same later.'

His voice shaking, Ranger told the rancher about the hollow on the ridge where Jack was hiding.

'I'm pretty sure he's telling the truth,' said Sinclair to the others. 'That Silver sure has a nerve, sitting up there and spying on us. You can go for him after midnight, Clem. Take three men with you. And I ain't too bothered about whether you bring him back dead or alive. Put Ranger back in that shed and make sure he's tied up good. We can let him go after we've got Silver.'

Because of the darkness, Jack had not observed the return of the Box S riders and their prisoner Ranger. He decided to stay where he was for the night, and before turning in he tethered the chestnut, already saddled as a precaution, at the bottom of the gully which ran from the hollow down the south side of the ridge.

Around one o'clock in the morning, he woke and listened intently for a while. There was a slight breeze blowing, but he could hear nothing which might indicate danger. Still uneasy, he threw off his blanket and sat up, reaching for his six-gun which was lying on the ground beside him.

Then, around the rim of the hollow, silhouetted against the night sky, four figures suddenly rose into view and ran down the slope towards Jack, firing their six-guns as they came. Lying down, in order to present a smaller target to the attackers, Jack fired at the man, a big man, who was nearest to him. His target, Clem Sinclair, went down. Several bullets had just missed Jack and when he saw Sinclair fall he swung his gun round to return the fire of the other attackers.

He saw one of them go down, then, almost immediately after, he was hit twice, once in the left arm and once in his side, just above the hip. He fired the remaining shots in his revolver at the two attackers still on their feet. They both sank down, one of them staggering backwards before he did so.

Jack rose to his feet, and crouching almost double and still under fire, he ran over to the gully running down the south side of the ridge. He disappeared into the gully without being hit again, and ignoring the pain in his side he scrambled down to his horse, climbed with some difficulty into the saddle, and rode off to the south, away from the valley.

Behind Jack, on top of the ridge, the Box S men were counting their losses. Only one of them was unhit. Clem Sinclair was dead, shot through the heart. One of the injured hands was shot in the chest and was incapable of riding. The other had been hit in the upper part of his leg. The uninjured hand decided that he'd better ride down alone to the ranch house for help.

Jack continued heading south, away from the valley. He heard no sounds of pursuit. He was sure he had hit at least two of the attackers, and while he was sure that Sinclair would continue the search for him, he guessed that pursuit would probably be delayed for a time. He decided to put as much distance as possible between himself and the valley before he stopped to take a look at his wounds.

Feeling his shirt and his pants as he rode along, he could tell that the clothing over the wounds was soaked with blood.

He rode on for just over an hour, when an attack of dizziness hit him and he was forced to dismount. He sat down on a boulder, pulled up his shirt sleeve, and felt the wound in his left arm, a little above the wrist. It was still bleeding, and the flesh felt badly torn, but the wound appeared to run along the surface and he doubted if there was a bullet lodged in the arm. He took off his bandanna, and holding one end between his teeth, he wound it tightly around the arm over the wound and tied it in position.

Then he investigated the second wound which he was sure was much more serious. He pulled his shirt out from inside the top of his pants and with his fingers he located the hole in the flesh where the bullet had penetrated his side. Blood was still coming from the wound. He was sure that the bullet was still inside him, and that he needed to see a doctor as quickly as possible.

He knew that there was a small town called Blair about thirteen miles south of his present position. Maybe there was a doctor there. With considerable difficulty, and groaning with the pain from his side, he dragged himself up into the saddle and headed south. As he proceeded, the pain in his side steadily worsened, and from time to time he almost lost consciousness, recovering just in time to avoid falling off his horse. He continued like this until daybreak, then paused for a short while to look ahead. There were no habitations in sight, but he was fairly certain that Blair was just beyond a distant ridge to the south.

He started moving again, and half a mile further on, as he was riding along the rim of a narrow, shallow ravine, he was forced to slow down when he came to a point where a portion of the wall of the ravine had collapsed. As he glanced downwards he heard a shout from below and stopped.

On the floor of the ravine a big horse was lying on its side, motionless. A man was trapped underneath the animal, which was pinning both his legs down. The man looked up at Jack. He was slim and middle-aged, and his face was drawn with pain.

'I sure am glad to see you, stranger,' he shouted. 'I figured I was going to cash in right here. I've tried, but I just can't get out from under this darned animal.'

'I'll be with you in a few minutes,' shouted Jack.

He rode back along the rim of the ravine until he reached a point where he could safely ride down into it. Then he rode along the rough floor of the ravine until he reached the fallen horse. He looked down at the man underneath it.

'Were you damaged much in the fall?' he asked.

'The ground at the the top of the slope there gave way,' said the man, 'and the horse and me both fell down here. When we hit the bottom the horse rolled over me once and we ended up like this. The horse had a broken leg and the way it was struggling to get up weren't doing me any good at all.

'I had to shoot it,' he went on. 'I don't feel too good inside. Maybe a rib or two's busted. But I think my legs'll be all right when I get them free. The name's Bracken, by the way, Dan Bracken.'

'Jack Silver,' said Jack. 'The first thing to do is get that horse off you.'

Slowly, he dismounted, and stood unsteadily by his horse for a moment, hanging on to the saddle pommel. Bracken looked up at Jack's face and the blood on his clothing.

'You don't look in too good a shape yourself,' he said.

'I've got a bullet in me,' said Jack. 'In the side. I was aiming to find me a doctor, but we can talk about that later.'

He took a rope from his horse and fastened one end around the dead horse's neck, and the other to the pommel of his own saddle. He paused, and spoke to Bracken.

'I'll do the best I can,' he said, 'But I reckon this is going to hurt some.'

'Go ahead,' said Bracken.

Jack took the reins of the powerful chestnut and urged it forward. He took a direction that he hoped would result in the dead horse being pulled off Bracken's legs without causing too much damage. Bracken yelled as the body slid over his feet. Jack stopped the chestnut and walked back to him.

'How d'you feel?' he asked.

Bracken slowly sat up, wincing as he did so. He

felt his body around the ribcage. Then he moved and flexed his legs and feet for a while before he stood up, swaying slightly.

'One ankle hurts some,' he said, 'but that's nothing. The main problem is that I reckon I've got some busted ribs. So I reckon we've *both* got to see a doctor.'

'Can you ride behind me?' asked Jack.

'I reckon so,' replied Bracken, 'if I can get up there.'

'Is there a doctor in Blair?' asked Jack.

'There is,' replied Bracken. 'Doc Gannon. I know him well. He's a good friend of ours.'

'We'd better ride there, then,' said Jack.

'I have a better idea,' said Bracken. 'My brother Ed and me, we're running a small ranch only three miles from here. That's a lot closer than Blair. We'll go there and Ed'll bring Doc Gannon to tend to us.'

'That sounds good,' said Jack. 'I don't know how much further I can ride.'

He walked with Bracken to a rock standing on the floor of the ravine and helped him to climb on to it. Then, painfully, he mounted the chestnut and rode up to the rock. Bracken lifted his leg over the horse and sat behind Jack, holding on to him around the chest. Then, riding slowly, they set off for the Bracken ranch, in a direction slightly west of south.

Just under an hour later, Bracken's sister-in-law, Jane, tending her small garden next to the ranch house, glanced to the north, then stood erect, staring at the big chestnut horse, unfamiliar to her, which had just appeared from behind the barn and was heading directly for her. Two men were sitting on the horse. Both were slumped forward and swaying a little as the horse approached her.

The woman ran to the door of the house and called out her husband Ed. He was a big man, just over six feet, and powerfully built. He ran after his wife to the horse, which had come to a halt, and they were just in time to support the two barely conscious riders as they started to slide off the horse's back. They eased them down to the ground.

When Dan Bracken and Jack came to they were lying on two beds in a small room at the back of the house, with Ed Bracken and his wife looking down at them. Dan told them about the horse falling on him, and Jack showed them the bullet-hole in his side.

'I'm going for Doc Gannon right now,' said Ed Bracken. 'I'll get him here as quick as I can.'

Jane Bracken made the two men as comfortable as possible while they waited for the doctor. When he arrived he took a quick look at Dan Bracken first, then inspected the wounds on Jack's arm and side.

'That bullet in your side's got to come out right away,' he said. 'The wound in the arm should heal up without any trouble.'

A few minutes later he started to probe in the wound for the bullet. By the time he had located it and pulled it out, Jack's face was beaded with perspiration. When the bullet was finally removed, he sank back on the bed with a great sigh of relief.

'You're a lucky man,' said the doctor. 'Now that I've got that bullet out, my guess is that the wound'll heal up without any trouble. I don't think there'll be any permanent damage. But that's only if you rest up for a while.'

He turned to Dan Bracken and gave him a detailed examination.

'Well, Dan,' he said, when he had finished. 'You've managed to get yourself a strained ankle and a busted rib. You're going to have to rest up for a spell. That pain you get when you breathe deep should go after a while. I'll put some bandaging around your ribs to make it a bit more comfortable for you. Then I'll be back in a couple of days to see how you're both doing.'

When they had seen the doctor off, Ed Bracken and his wife came back into the room where Jack and Dan were lying. Dan looked over towards Jack.

'I sure was glad you happened by this morning,' he said. 'If it hadn't been for you I could've been stuck under that horse for days. I'd been up to Amarillo on business and Ed and Jane here didn't know when to expect me back.'

Jack told them how it came about that he was riding through the area with a bullet inside him.

'I've heard of Sinclair,' said Ed Bracken. 'D'you think he'll carry on chasing you?'

'I'm sure of it,' replied Jack. He would have been doubly sure, had he known that one of his shots, up

on the ridge, had killed Clem Sinclair, the rancher's
only remaining son.

'What I'm worried about,' he went on, 'is that
Sinclair's men might follow me here and start causing you trouble. If he's got a good tracker in his
outfit, maybe he could follow my trail. I lost a fair
amount of blood on the way here and I wasn't up to
doing anything about hiding my tracks. I'm going to
ride on right now. If you can manage it, I'd be glad
of a few provisions to take with me.'

Jack started to rise from the bed, but Ed placed a
large hand on his chest and gently pushed him back.

'You're staying right where you are,' he said.
'When d'you reckon those Box S men might show
up here?'

'Maybe tomorrow,' said Jack. 'They couldn't take
off after me right away. I know I hit two of them last
night, maybe three. But I still think I should move
on now. I don't want nobody here to get hurt.'

Once again he tried to rise and once again Ed
gently pushed him back.

'We can't let you go,' said Ed, 'especially after
what you did for Dan here. You ain't fit to ride.'

'All right,' said Jack. 'If you're set on me staying
here I have an idea that might work.'

'Let's hear it,' said Ed.

'Is there any place here where I could hide from
Sinclair's men if they do show up?' asked Jack.

Ed pondered for a while before he replied.

'The best place,' he said, 'would be the storeroom
Dan and me dug out under the living-room before

we put the floorboards down. There's a trapdoor in the floor and some steps below it. We can lay a rug over the trapdoor to hide it.'

'That sounds just right,' said Jack. 'The next thing we need is for you to dig a grave on the top of that knoll near the house and fill it in again.'

Puzzled, they stared at him.

'I aim to try and make Sinclair believe I'm dead,' he explained, 'so that he'll stop chasing me for a while. The story I'd like you to tell his men is that I turned up here with Dan, just like it actually happened, but say that I had a bullet lodged near the heart and that I died when the doctor was trying to get it out. So you buried me up on the knoll. You can show them my horse. I'm sure they'll recognize it.'

'The other thing that's got to be done,' Jack went on, 'is for Doc Gannon to be asked to say that I died while he was trying to dig that bullet out. D'you think he'll be willing to do that?'

'There ain't no doubt about it when he knows what's at stake,' said Ed. 'I'll start digging on the knoll now, and I'll keep an eye open for riders coming from the north, just in case. When I've done that I'll ride into town to see the doctor.'

While Ed Bracken was digging, his wife got Jack's hiding place ready for him to use, if need be. When Ed returned to the house some time later, he told them that the grave had been dug and filled in again, and that a rough wooden cross had been driven into the ground close to it.

When, later on, he returned from town, he told them that Doc Gannon had agreed to cooperate.

'That's good,' said Jack. 'I figure that Sinclair's men might pay him a visit to check on your story.'

FIVE

The following day, Ed Bracken and his wife took turns in watching for riders coming from the north, but it was early afternoon before Ed spotted seven horsemen heading towards him. He called to his wife and she helped Jack down into the hiding place under the floor, then replaced the trapdoor and rug. Ed came in and waited with his wife until the riders were coming to a stop outside the house. Then they both stepped outside.

One rider was slightly ahead of the others. From Jack's description Ed felt pretty sure that this was Jed Sinclair, owner of the Box S. The other riders were a tough-looking bunch, all armed.

'Howdy,' said Ed.

Sinclair ignored the greeting. There was a ruthless look on his face as his eyes bored into Ed's.

'I'm looking for a man called Jack Silver,' he said. 'We followed his trail here. He's wounded.' He glanced over at the corral. 'That big chestnut,' he said, 'that looks like the horse he was riding. Silver's a murderer. Just hand him over and nobody'll get hurt.'

'That just ain't going to be possible,' said Ed. 'This Silver helped my brother when his horse rolled over him a few miles north of here. Maybe you saw the dead horse?'

Sinclair nodded.

'When Silver got here he was near finished,' said Ed. 'There was a bullet in him, close to the heart. We got Doc Gannon to come out from Blair, and while he was poking around for the bullet Silver cashed in. We buried him on top of the hill over there.'

He pointed to the small cross, just visible at the top of the knoll.

Sinclair spoke to his men.

'Search the house and the other buildings,' he said, 'and search them good. One of you keep these two covered. And you, Purvis, go and take a closer look at that chestnut.'

He turned his horse and rode up to the top of the knoll. He dismounted and stood looking down at the grave for a while. On his face was a look of grim satisfaction.

By the time he rode down to the house his men had finished their search.

'That's Silver's horse all right,' said Purvis, 'and there's a sick man inside the house, but he ain't Silver.' He pointed to Ed and his wife. 'These two and the sick man inside are the only folks here.'

'We'll ride into Blair,' said Sinclair, 'and have a word with that doctor before we ride back to the Box S.'

Jane Bracken helped Jack up from below as soon as the seven riders had disappeared from view, and he rejoined Dan Bracken in the bedroom. Ed came in shortly after.

'I had a bad time,' he said, 'when Sinclair was standing on top of the knoll there. I was expecting that any minute he'd call on his men to dig down into that grave. But it looks like he swallowed my story.'

'I ain't surprised,' smiled his wife, 'seeing as you're one of the best liars I know.'

'That's true,' grinned Dan.

'I'm a bit worried,' said Jack, 'about what Sinclair'll do about taking over the Carson ranch now he thinks I'm dead. I'm hoping the Carsons'll stay in Bridger for the time being. They should be safe there. What I've got to do is ride back there as soon as I'm able. I'm expecting two friends of mine to turn up there before long.'

'Don't rush it,' said Jane Bracken. 'You want to be fit before you face up to that man Sinclair again. He looked a real villain to me.'

The doctor called the following day. He said that Sinclair had been to see him and that he had sent the rancher on his way, satisfied that Jack was dead. Jack thanked him, and after Gannon had examined his wounds, he asked him when he would be fit to ride again.

'Everything's healing up fine,' said the doctor, 'but you need at least ten days before you climb on a horse again. You'd be a fool to leave any earlier.'

He went on to look at Dan Bracken, and pronounced himself satisfied with his progress.

Ten days later, Jack thanked the Brackens and headed north. He had ridden about five miles when he was aware of a rider on a similar course to his own, overhauling him from behind. He turned, and watched the other rider as he approached. He was a stocky, middle-aged man riding a good-looking bay horse. He smiled as he came up to Jack and stopped in front of him.

'Howdy, stranger,' he said. 'I see we're both heading the same way. Maybe we can ride along together for a spell. I sure am tired of my own company. I'm Brad Jordan.'

'Jack Silver,' said Jack. 'Glad to have you along.'

He turned, and they rode along, side by side.

'I'm heading for the ranch I run with my brother Al,' said Jordan. 'It's about four miles from here. I've been away a couple of weeks, finding a buyer for our horses.'

'You're breeding horses?' asked Jack.

'That's right,' replied Jordan. 'There's a big demand from ranchers just now for good quarter horses. We've got around fifty head at the ranch just now, waiting to be collected.'

Forty minutes later, Jordan stopped as they came to a point on some high ground from which they could look down into a narrow valley. Jack followed suit. A stream ran through the valley and some horses were grazing along its banks. To the right, half a mile away, was a small cluster of buildings and a large, empty corral.

'That's it,' said Jordan. 'That's the ranch.'

Proudly, he ran his eye over the spread. Then he stiffened.

'There's something wrong,' he said. 'There's a lot of horses missing.'

He rode quickly down the slope into the valley and headed for the house. Jack followed him. When Jordan reached the house he dismounted and ran inside, calling his brother's name. Shortly after, he came out, then visited each of the other buildings in turn. Finally, he came back to Jack, who had dismounted.

'Al ain't here,' he said, 'and I'm pretty sure them fifty quarter horses I just got a buyer for ain't here either.'

As Jack looked around his eye was caught by what looked like a body lying at the bottom of the corral fence. Jordan saw it at the same time and started running towards it. Jack followed him. When he came up to Jordan, the rancher, white-faced, was standing motionless, staring down at the body of a man lying face upwards on the ground. From the state of the body, it must have been lying there for some time. There was a bullet-hole in the middle of the forehead.

'It's Al,' said Jordan, hoarsely. He was obviously badly shaken. 'Looks like whoever took the horses killed him.'

'How long is it since you left here?' asked Jack.

'Twelve days.' replied Jordan.

'Then it looks like your brother died soon after

you left,' said Jack, 'and I think I know who might have killed him.'

Jordan stared at him. 'You do?' he asked.

Jack nodded, then went on to tell Jordan about Sinclair's threats against the Carsons and how the rancher had followed him to the Bracken ranch after his two sons had been killed. He told Jordan that he was riding back to the valley where the Box S ranch was located, in order to help the Carsons in their fight against Sinclair.

'Just around the time your brother was killed,' he said, 'Sinclair and his men were riding back from Blair to the Box S. They would be passing close by your place. Sinclair's a greedy man and a ruthless one, and he hates small ranchers. It wouldn't surprise me if when he saw those quarter horses as he was passing by, he decided he had to have them. And when your brother got in the way, they shot him.

'I can't be absolutely sure of it,' he concluded, 'but I reckon that Sinclair's responsible for what happened here.'

Jordan's face hardened as he looked down at his dead brother.

'I'd like to ride with you, if you don't mind waiting till I've buried Al,' he said. 'I'm going to send a message to my other brother Jesse in Fort Worth to tell him about Al, and ask him to come and look after the ranch for a spell while I find out if it really was Sinclair and his men who were here.'

'You can send that message by telegraph when we

get to Bridger,' said Jack. 'I reckon you'd recognize your horses if you saw them, wouldn't you?'

'I sure would,' said Jordan.

'Then if you spot them on the Box S, that'll be the proof that you need,' said Jack.

They buried Al on a slope facing the front of the house, then Jack continued on his way, Jordan riding by his side. Night had fallen by the time they rode down into the valley and headed for Bridger. They left their horses in the thicket outside town and, keeping off the main street, they approached the store from the rear. Jack knocked on the door, which was opened by Emily Drury.

She seemed completely taken aback at the sight of him and it was a moment before she could speak.

'We all thought you were dead,' she said. 'Come inside.'

'Are the Carsons all right?' asked Jack as he and Jordan stepped in.

'Yes,' she said. 'They're all here, in the living-room. Come on through.'

As they entered, Jack saw the Carsons and Drury seated at a table. They had obviously just finished a meal. Seeing Jack, they all sat rigid for a moment, as though they were seeing a ghost. Mary paled for a moment, then gave a great gasp of relief.

'It sure is good to see you, Jack,' said Carson. 'We had it straight from Sinclair's own mouth that you were lying in a grave somewhere this side of Blair. He claimed he'd actually seen the grave.'

'He saw what looked like a grave,' said Jack, 'but I

didn't happen to be in it. Have my friends Tex Foster and Milt Grayson turned up yet?'

'No,' replied Carson.

Jack introduced Brad Jordan to the others and they all sat down, Jack taking a seat next to Mary. Then the others listened as Jack gave an account of events since he had last seen them. When he had finished there was silence for a moment. Then Carson spoke.

'Sinclair's taken our ranch buildings over,' he said. 'Two of his men are living there. He says they'll shoot us if we show up anywhere near. And he's made me another offer for the ranch. I said I wasn't interested in moving, not at any price, but he said he'd give me a couple of weeks to think it over, and if I didn't accept his offer by then, I'd be very sorry.'

'What about your hands Randle and Ranger?' asked Jack.

'They're both in town,' replied Carson. 'Ranger was taken by Sinclair's men before you were shot. They threatened him with a red-hot branding iron and he was forced to tell them where you were hiding out. He's been feeling really bad about it. He's going to be mighty relieved when he finds out you ain't dead.'

'I wondered how Sinclair knew where I was,' said Jack, 'but I don't blame Ranger for telling him. I know what devilry Sinclair's capable of.'

As he finished speaking they heard a knock on the rear door. Jack rose to his feet and drew his six-gun, as Drury got up to go to the door.

'I'll come with you,' said Jack, 'just in case Sinclair's men are paying you a call.'

As Drury opened the door Jack took up a position behind it.

'Mr Drury?' asked the man outside.

'That's me,' said the storekeeper.

'My name's Tex Foster,' said the man outside. 'I was hoping to find an old friend of mine called Jack Silver here.'

'You've found him, Mr Foster,' said Drury. 'Come inside.'

As Tex stepped inside, the storekeeper closed the door behind him, and Jack walked up to his friend and former deputy.

'Thanks for coming, Tex,' he said. 'I sent a message to Milt as well, but he ain't turned up yet. I figure he'll be here soon.'

'Sorry I'm a mite late, Jack,' said the newcomer. 'I wasn't in Santa Fe when your message arrived there, but as soon as I got it I headed out here.'

Tex was a big, powerful-looking man, a little taller than Jack, and bearded, with thick black hair falling down to his collar. He wore a right-hand gun, and a knife on his belt. There was a cheerful look about him, as he smiled at his friend.

'Come and meet the others,' said Jack.

They went into the living-room and, after making the introductions, Jack described the situation to Tex.

'This man Sinclair,' said Tex, when Jack had finished, 'has obviously got to be stopped. You got a plan?'

'Now that I've got you and Brad here to help me,' said Jack, 'I'm sure we can work something out.'

He thought for a moment, then continued.

'It's not easy to get at Sinclair,' he said, 'because of all the men he has on his payroll. I've been working on this idea of us grabbing his men in ones and twos whenever we get the chance, and hiding them somewhere outside the valley, not too far away. Question is, where could that somewhere be? Has anybody got any ideas?'

Carson and Drury pondered over the question, then both shook their heads.

'You want some place,' said Carson, 'where they can be properly fastened in without any chance of them breaking out. I can't think of one off-hand. But if you *could* capture some of Sinclair's men, what would your next move be?'

'The next move,' said Jack, 'would be to capture Sinclair himself and take him to the nearest US marshal, with all the proof necessary to get him convicted for the crimes he's committed up to now.'

'Just a minute!' said Tex. 'About that place where the Box S men could be held. On my ride here from Santa Fe, not long before I crossed over from New Mexico Territory into Texas, I passed by what was left of an old Army fort that weren't all that far from here. It was roughly due west of where we are now. It looked like it had been burned down long ago, probably by Indians, but one brick-built building was still standing.

'It was the guardhouse,' he went on. 'As it

happens, I had a look inside it, and I reckon it would be possible to hold maybe up to fifteen prisoners in there if we took a strong padlock and chain along.'

'I could supply that,' said Drury.

'It was right in the middle of nowhere,' Tex went on, 'and it looked like nobody had been around there for a long time. What d'you think?'

'Sounds like just the right place,' said Jack. 'You and me'll ride along there during the night and have a look at it come daylight tomorrow, to see if we can make it secure.'

'I'd like to go along,' said Jordan.

'Sure,' said Jack.

'If it looks right for the job,' said Tex, 'somebody'll have to stay on guard there all the time as soon as we get any prisoners.'

'I think that maybe Hank Randle and Josh Ranger would want to help out with the guarding,' said Carson. 'Particularly Josh. He feels pretty bad about telling Sinclair about Jack's hiding-place on the ridge.'

'That would be good,' said Jack. 'It would leave three of us to concentrate on picking up Sinclair's hands.'

SIX

The three men left the store after eating a meal which Emily and Mary prepared for them, and after Brad had given Carson a message to be sent by telegraph to his brother Jesse. As they were leaving, Jack told Mary and the others that they would be coming back to the store the following evening.

They rode west up the valley, staying well clear of the Box S buildings, and as dawn was breaking they rode up to the ruins of the fort which Tex had told them about. Jack could see that it had been a large fort, built without a stockade. For some reason, no attempt had been made to rebuild it after its destruction. They headed for the guardhouse, dismounted, and inspected it inside and out.

It was a detached building, with thick walls constructed of brick, and a flat timber roof made of thick wooden beams laid across the tops of two opposite walls. The brickwork and timber were still in reasonable condition, although the roof timbers were slightly charred. In the wall facing into the

square were three windows, two of which were heavily barred.

The door into the guardhouse led first into a small
room with a window, small fireplace and chimney.
From this room a door led into a second room
containing a large cell, with two barred windows,
Access to the cell was via a door constructed of a
metal framework with vertical iron bars. Built into
one end wall of the cell were a small fireplace and
chimney.

Jack closely examined the door of the cell. It was
in good condition, but the key used for securing it
was missing. He walked over to look at the two cell
windows. The bars were firmly set in the brickwork.

'This cell looks pretty secure,' he said. 'All we need
is a strong chain and a padlock to hold the door. And
whoever's guarding the prisoners can live in the
other room.'

They walked out of the guardhouse, and Brad
walked over to what looked like the remains of a
structure normally provided at the top of a well shaft.
Looking down he could see that the shaft was still
intact, and when he dropped a stone he heard the
faint sound of a splash as it hit water. He returned to
the others.

'Should be all right for water,' he said.

'That's good,' said Jack. 'I reckon this place is just
what we want. We can't do any more here now.
Before it's dark I want to get back to that lookout I
used on the ridge overlooking the Box S ranch
house.'

When they reached the valley they rode along the south side of the ridge that Jack had referred to, then climbed up the gully into the hollow on top of the ridge, from which they could look down on the Box S. All three of them lay down on the lip of the hollow and looked down towards the ranch buildings.

There were no men in sight, either on foot or in the saddle, but Jack's eye was caught by a herd of horses grazing in the pasture. He studied the horses for a short while, then handed his field-glasses to Brad.

'Those horses in the pasture,' he said. 'Do any of them look familiar to you?'

Brad took the glasses, trained them on the pasture, and almost immediately he stiffened.

'Damn Sinclair,' he said. 'I can see three quarter horses already that were stolen from our ranch. There's a pinto, a bay and a golden chestnut.'

He paused for a moment, then continued.

'I'm with you all the way,' he said, grimly. 'That murderer down there has got to be stopped. I ain't no gunfighter, but I reckon I can handle a six-gun and a rifle pretty well, and I ain't scared to use them.'

'Right,' said Jack. 'Let's get a few hours' sleep here, then we'll ride in to Bridger and start getting ourselves organized against Sinclair.'

They reached Bridger around midnight, and entered the store from the rear. The Carsons and Drurys had stayed up, awaiting their arrival. Jack told them that the old guardhouse was suitable for their purpose, and that they planned to start the operation against Sinclair as soon as they could.

'I spoke to Ranger and Randle,' said Carson, 'and they both want to help you as much as they can. They've always done a good job for me on the ranch, and they're as keen as I am that Sinclair should be stopped from taking it over.'

'That's good,' said Jack. 'We sure can use them.'

'And what about me?' asked Carson. 'What can I do to help?'

'It's best for you to stay here in town,' said Jack. 'Then Sinclair can't suspect you when his men start to go missing.'

He turned to Drury.

'Mr Drury,' he asked, 'do any Box S men ever come into town alone?'

'Only one,' replied Drury. 'He's a man called Derry. He's a big, burly man with a pock-marked face, always wearing a gun. He visits the saloon most evenings. Comes in here sometimes for tobacco and ammunition. He rides a big grey horse.'

'He can be our first prisoner, then,' said Jack, 'and the next ones can be the two men who are occupying the Carson ranch.

'You stay in town tonight, Brad,' he went on, 'and tomorrow hire a packhorse and take plenty of supplies and a chain and padlock, and anything else you think we might need, out to the guardhouse. Then wait for us to come along with the prisoner. Tex and I'll go out now to the hiding place on the ridge. We'll stay there during daylight and come back here after dark.'

'Maybe my two hands Ranger and Randle could

ride out to the guardhouse with Mr Jordan,'
suggested Carson.

'That's a good idea,' said Jack. 'They'll be needed
there soon. But they'll have to be sure that nobody
from the Box S spots them on the way. And it might
be a good idea to put it around that they quit, and
have ridden south to look for work.'

'I'll see to that,' said Carson.

A little later, Jack and Tex departed, and reached
the hollow on the ridge while it was still dark. They
slept awhile, then rose shortly after dawn and kept
watch on the Box S ranch buildings below. There was
no unusual activity. A few hands were busying themselves in and around the buildings, and early in the
day several hands rode out on the range in different
directions and disappeared from the watchers' view.
They returned in the late afternoon.

After dark, Jack and Tex headed for Bridger.
Leaving their horses outside town, they walked on
to the store, taking care not to be seen. Mrs Drury
let them in and took them through to the Carsons
in the living-room. Her husband was working in the
store.

Carson told them that Brad Jordan, with Randle
and Ranger, had left for the guardhouse around
noon, with a packhorse loaded with all the necessi-
ties for a stay of some time. They were all three going
to wait at the abandoned fort until Jack and Tex
arrived.

'Do you know if Derry from the Box S is in town
this evening?' Jack asked Carson.

'I don't know,' replied the rancher. 'I'll go and see if he's in the saloon.'

He went out, and returned a few minutes later.

'He's in there,' he said, 'sitting at a table by himself. From what George told me, he should be there another hour or so. He always leaves around ten.'

Jack and Tex had a quick meal, chatting with Mary and her parents as they ate. Then they left by the back door and walked back to the thicket where their horses were tethered. The trail from town to the Box S skirted this thicket. They stood just inside the thicket, waiting. Jack was holding a lariat, the loop in his right hand and the remaining coils in his left.

Just under half an hour had passed before they heard the sound of an approaching horse, moving quite slowly. They let it pass by, then Jack stepped silently out behind it. He could see the horse and rider clearly outlined against the night sky. Running after them he made an overhand toss for the rider's head, then jerked the loop tight around his body, pinning his arms to his sides. A heave on the rope brought his victim crashing to the ground, where Tex relieved him of his gun and tied his hands with a piece of rope.

Jack struck a match and looked at the man's face. It fitted Drury's description of Derry exactly. He knew they had caught the right man. On seeing Jack's face by the light of the match, Derry started.

'You're Silver,' he said. 'You're supposed to be dead. What're you aiming to do with me?'

'You're going on a longish ride,' said Jack. 'Try and get away, and we'll shoot you down.'

He went for Derry's horse, which had run on a little way, and brought it back to Tex and the prisoner.

'Mount up,' he said to Derry, and the three riders rode up the valley in single file, with the prisoner in the middle. Giving the Box S ranch buildings a wide berth, they rode to the head of the valley, then on to the fort, which they reached at sun-up. Randle, who was on watch, called Brad Jordan and Ranger, who came out of the guardhouse as Jack and the others stopped outside.

'First instalment?' asked Brad.

'That's right,' replied Jack. 'Everything all right here?'

'Sure,' replied Brad. 'We've cleaned the place up a bit and collected plenty of firewood, and we're all ready to take in anybody you want to bring along.'

'This man's called Derry,' said Jack, pointing to the prisoner. 'You can take him inside.'

Brad told the prisoner to dismount. Then he cut the rope binding Derry's hands and took him through to the cell, followed by Jack and Tex. Derry cursed as he realized that he was about to be held prisoner in the cell, but Brad prodded him into it with the barrel of his six-gun, then closed the door behind the prisoner and secured it with the stout chain and padlock they had brought out from Bridger.

'This ain't lawful!' shouted Derry, 'locking me up like this.'

'You work for Jed Sinclair,' said Jack, 'and he ain't exactly a law-abiding man. So I ain't bothered too much about keeping you prisoner here. We figure to have some of your friends along to keep you company soon.'

Followed by a volley of curses from Derry, Jack and the others left the guardhouse and stood talking outside.

'Has anybody passed by since you got here?' asked Jack.

'Nary a soul,' replied Brad. 'There ain't much of a reason for anybody to come this way.'

'Good,' said Jack. 'Let's hope it stays that way.'

'What's your next move?' asked Brad.

'Tex and me, we're going to get some sleep right now,' replied Jack, 'and tonight we'll ride back to the valley and see if we can pick up those two Box S hands from the Carson ranch house.'

'You need any help?' asked Brad.

'I reckon the two of us can do the job,' replied Jack. 'It's best if all three of you stay here for now.'

Jack and Tex slept until mid-afternoon. Then they had a quick meal and left for the valley.

'If all goes well,' said Jack as they were leaving, 'we'll be back early tomorrow morning.'

It was dark before they reached the valley and started riding down it towards the Carson ranch. Later, as they approached the ranch buildings, they could see a light coming from inside the two-storey house. They dismounted, tethered their horses behind the barn, and watched the light until, just after eleven o'clock, it went out.

They waited an hour, then walked over to the house and tried the door. It was not barred. Jack opened it slowly and the two men entered and stood listening for a short while. Then Jack struck a match and lit a small oil lamp which stood on a nearby table. He took hold of the lamp and walked across the room to the bottom of the staircase leading to the upper part of the house. Tex was close behind him. They paused and listened. They could hear the faint sound of snoring floating down from above.

Jack turned the lamp well down and slowly climbed the stairs, followed by Tex. A passage at the top of the stairs led to the closed doors of two bedrooms. The snores were coming from the room behind the first door. They could hear no noise from the room behind the second door, indicating either that it was empty, or that it contained a silent sleeper.

They returned to the first door, opened it, closed it behind them, and quickly walked over to a bed on which a man was lying, fast asleep. Jack placed the lamp on the bedside table and, as the sleeper showed signs of waking up, Jack tapped him on the forehead with the barrel of his Colt .45.

As the ranch hand, a man called Bradley, started to rise, he saw the gun in Jack's hand. Tex forced a gag into his mouth and tied it tightly at the back of his neck. Then he tied the man hand and foot and roped him to the bed.

Leaving their victim lying on the bed, Tex and Jack entered the second bedroom and found another

Box S hand called Watkins sleeping peacefully there. They woke him up and tied his hands, then took him into the other bedroom.

'What's all this about?' he asked.

'You're trespassing,' said Jack. 'This property belongs to John Carson. That's why we're taking you and your friend here to spend a spell in jail.'

'Where?' shouted Watkins. 'You can't do that. You ain't the law.'

'Shut up!' said Jack, 'or we'll gag you.'

Tex took the gag off Bradley and untied his feet, then they all went downstairs.

'Wait here with them, Tex,' said Jack, 'while I get their horses.'

He found the horses in the pasture, and their saddles and bridles in the barn. He saddled the two mounts and led them to the house, then went to collect his own horse and Tex's from behind the barn.

They set off for the old fort immediately, but in order to confuse any pursuers they headed first for the river, then rode through the shallows near the river bank until they left the river on to hard ground near the head of the valley. Then they headed for the fort.

They reached it about an hour after dawn, and handed the prisoners over to Brad and the others. After Bradley and Watkins had been put in the cell with Derry, Jack talked with Brad outside the guard-house.

'Did you have any trouble with Derry?' he asked.

'There was a lot of bad language coming from in there,' said Brad, ''till I threatened to stop feeding him. Apart from that he ain't given us no trouble.'

'I ain't quite sure yet,' said Jack, 'just where we're going to hit Sinclair next, but I have an idea that might work and likely we'll need your help. Would you ride to that hide-out on top of the ridge overlooking the Box S buildings? And be there by dawn tomorrow?'

'Sure I will,' said Brad.

Jack spoke to Ranger and Randle.

'Are you men happy about guarding these prisoners on your own?' he asked.

'Sure,' said Ranger. 'You don't need to worry about us.' Randle nodded agreement.

As on the previous day, Jack and Tex had a meal and slept for a few hours before they headed back for the valley and Bridger. They reached the head of the valley before sunset and stayed there for a while, awaiting the fall of darkness. Looking down into the valley, Jack could see a large, grassy, steep-sided basin which contained a number of cows. He examined it closely through his field-glasses. He counted around 120 head, and noticed that ropes had been stretched across the only gap, between two large boulders, which allowed easy access to the basin for cattle.

He wondered why this small group of cattle had been taken off the range to be assembled at that point. Perhaps, he thought, a buyer was due to pick them up in the near future. As he looked at the cows, he decided on a plan for his next move against Sinclair.

When they reached Bridger they left their horses outside town and entered the store from the rear again. Inside, they told Carson and the others of the capture and jailing of the three Box S hands.

'Sinclair don't know what to make of it all,' said Carson. 'His men have searched the town, as well as the range and the ridges on both sides of the valley, for the missing men. They came in here twice this afternoon. I reckon he's a very puzzled man. He didn't even mention the business of us leaving the valley, but he did warn us not to go back to the ranch house.

'I have some bad news for you,' Carson went on. 'Although you took three of Sinclair's men, he took on two new hands today from a trail crew passing through here on their way back to Texas.'

'Bad news, as you say,' said Jack, 'but it just makes the job a bit longer, that's all. Don't think of going back to the ranch. There's no point in risking trouble with Sinclair just now. We're hoping to give him something else to occupy his mind with in the next few days.

'I guess there's no sign of Milt Grayson yet?' he added.

'No,' replied Carson. 'Maybe he'd moved on before your message reached him.'

'Maybe,' said Jack, 'but I'm sure he'll turn up sometime.'

Jack and Tex had a meal, then prepared to leave,

Jack saying that it might be a few days before they were in Bridger again. Mary accompanied Jack to the door.

'I guess it ain't going to be so easy for you now that Sinclair's expecting trouble,' she said.

Jack smiled at her. 'That's right,' he said. 'But I still think we can keep one step ahead of him and stop him from taking your ranch over.'

'I think you know how grateful we are to you all,' she said, 'and you must know that every time you leave here we're sick with worry that you won't be back again.'

'We'll be back,' said Jack, as he opened the door, and he and Tex sidled out into the darkness.

'That's a nice girl,' said Tex, as they walked away from the store.

'I ain't arguing that,' said Jack.

'I reckon she'd make a fine wife for the right man,' said Tex.

'I'm hoping,' said Jack to his old friend, 'that once this is all over maybe I'll get the chance to see how she feels about us getting married and settling down somewhere.'

'Considering the way she looks at you,' said Tex, 'I figure there ain't no doubt that you'd get the answer you want.'

As they walked out of town to pick up their horses, Jack discussed with Tex his plan for the next move against Sinclair.

They rode right up the valley until they reached the basin in which they had seen the Box S cattle earlier in the day. They removed the ropes across the entrance to the basin, then rode inside it and along to the far end. As they passed through the herd the cows rose to their feet.

Tex and Jack started driving the cattle out of the basin and up the slope, gentle at that point, of the ridge which bordered the valley to the south. They carried on down the far slope of the ridge and drove the cattle in a southerly direction, as fast as they could urge them along, for a distance of around four miles. Then they left the cows and rode back, as fast as they were able, towards the valley. Arriving at the ridge they had recently crossed over with the cows, they rode along its foot until they came to the gully leading up to the hollow on top of the ridge. As they rode into the gully they spotted a horse which was hidden by some foliage from the view of anyone looking towards the gully from the south. Jack looked closely at the animal.

'Brad's horse,' he said. 'He's here.'

They dismounted, tethered their horses close to Brad's, then started walking up the gully. Dawn was just breaking. As they neared the top Jack called out, and shortly after Brad appeared above them, a six-gun in his hand.

'Figured it was you two,' he said, 'when I heard somebody climbing up here.'

Jack and Tex walked up into the hollow and sat down with Brad to eat some food they had brought with them. They told him of their activities over the past few hours and of the reasons for their presence on the top of the ridge.

'That's quite a plan you dreamed up,' said Brad.
'Let's hope it works,' said Jack.

SEVEN

The three men on top of the ridge kept the Box S buildings under observation all day. Around eight o'cock in the morning a party led by Sinclair and numbering seven men, rode off at speed down the valley, presumably to continue the search for the missing hands.

So far as the watchers could tell there were still three ranch hands down below, plus the cook, who several times appeared briefly outside the cook-shack. One of the hands rode off down the valley just before noon, and another rode up the valley early in the afternoon.

The party led by Sinclair returned an hour before sunset, at the same time as the ranch hand who had earlier ridden down the valley. They had all barely had time to dismount when the ranch hand who had, a few hours ago, ridden up the valley, rode up to them at speed. He dismounted and ran over to Sinclair.

Watching from above, Jack and the others sensed Sinclair's anger as he barked orders to his men.

Nine fresh horses were saddled and the cook brought out packets of food for the men. Within half an hour of Sinclair's arrival eight men, led by the rancher, were heading up the valley at speed.

'Our luck's in,' said Jack. 'It's clear that Sinclair's been told about the missing cattle and he's going to chase after the rustlers. I figure there are three men down there, including the cook. Maybe we could have managed four, but three'll do. We'll sneak down there as soon as it's dark and take them prisoner.'

Half an hour later, they rode down the side of the ridge and headed for the ranch buildings. Leaving their horses behind a large shed, well away from the other buildings, they looked towards the house, then the bunkhouse and cookshack. The only building showing a light was the cookshack.

They checked the house and bunkhouse to make sure there was no one inside, then all three advanced on the cookshack. Standing outside, near the door, they could hear the sound of voices coming from inside. Looking through a window Jack could see two men seated at a table and the cook standing by the stove.

Quietly, gun in hand, he moved along to the door, opened it and walked into the shack, with Tex and Brad, also armed, close behind him. The cook was the first to see them. He froze, with a pan in his hand, and the two men at the table, seeing the look on his face, swivelled round on their seats to look up into the grim faces of three armed men. Tex moved up behind them to take their guns.

'My name is Silver,' said Jack. 'You men are going for a ride just as soon as we have mounts ready for you. And don't think of trying any tricks. We don't need much of an excuse to shoot you down.'

'Mr Sinclair ain't going to like this,' said one of the men. 'You're going to be sorry when he catches up with you.'

'That prospect don't bother us none,' said Jack. He spoke to Tex and Brad. 'I'll watch these three,' he said, 'while you go and rustle up mounts for them.'

He pointed to a big oil lamp standing on the floor.

'Light that lamp and take it with you,' he said.

When Tex and Brad had left, Jack spoke to the cook, who was still standing by the stove.

'Where you men are going to stay for a while,' he said, 'grub ain't all that easy to come by. So you'd better fill a couple of sacks with provisions and we'll take them along with us. I wouldn't want you three to starve.'

As the cook, a scared look on his face, busied himself placing provisions in two sacks, Jack watched him and the two hands at the table. The two seated men looked more mad than scared. They didn't look like typical cowhands, and Jack guessed that Sinclair had hired them more for their gun-handling than for their cow-handling abilities.

After a while one of the two hands at the table, a tall, thin man with cold eyes and a straggly, drooping moustache, started to rise to his feet, but sank down again abruptly as a bullet from Jack's Peacemaker passed within an inch of his right ear and struck a large pan hanging from a hook on the wall. The pan, jerked off the hook by the impact, clattered to the floor.

'I don't remember saying you could get up,' said Jack.

Moments later Tex and Brad ran in, with guns drawn. They holstered them when they saw that Jack was still in control.

'We've got the horses outside,' said Tex.

'Right,' said Jack. 'Tie their hands in front of them and search them for any hidden weapons, then we'll be on our way.'

When this had been done the three Box S men were taken outside and were ordered to mount. The sacks of provisions were tied on to two of the horses and the three prisoners started riding up the valley, each of them led by one of their captors. Jack took a route which led across the ridge before the head of the valley was reached, so as to remove any danger of meeting up with Sinclair and his party. He also took a route across terrain over which tracks would be very difficult to follow. The journey passed without incident, and it was still well before dawn when they arrived at the old fort.

Jack went ahead, to warn Randle and Ranger of their arrival. He rapped on the door of the guard-house and called out his name. Randle, a shotgun in his hand, opened it a few moments later.

'Everything all right here?' asked Jack.

'Everything's fine,' replied Randle.

'We've brought another three prisoners,' said Jack, then rode back to bring the others up to the guardhouse. They ordered the prisoners to dismount and took them through to the cell. They were prodded inside and the cell door was secured behind them. Jack spoke to the three men already inside.

'You men are in luck,' he said. 'Like you see, we've brought your own cook along to help you out.'

A burst of profanity rose inside the cell as Jack and the others went through into the other room, closing the door behind them. Jack told Randle and Ranger of the trick played on Sinclair which had enabled them to take three more prisoners.

'I reckon Sinclair's down to six hands now,' he went on. 'He sure must be mighty puzzled about where they've gone, and who took them. Trouble is, he'll be well on his guard now after losing six men. If we could split them up somehow, maybe we could capture more of his men, maybe even Sinclair himself.'

'I've been nursing an idea for a while,' said Tex. 'You know that nobody at the Box S or in town, apart from the Carsons and the Drurys, has seen me before. What if I ride up to the Box S and ask for a job as a ranch hand? Sinclair being short-handed, most likely he'd take me on, and maybe I'd get the chance to capture him without his men knowing about it and take him to the fort.'

'I reckon,' said Jack, 'that Sinclair will really be on

the lookout for trouble right now, and what you're thinking of doing would be too dangerous for yourself. But I have another idea that might work if Sinclair took you on.'

They discussed Jack's plan at length and decided to go ahead with it.

'We'll rest up today,' said Jack, 'then Tex, Brad and myself'll ride to the valley overnight.'

He asked Randle and Ranger if they could keep on guarding the prisoners without any help.

'Sure,' replied Ranger. 'They've plenty of food and water inside the cell to last them quite a while yet, and whenever Hank and me are anywhere near them we carry a loaded shotgun. That's something I don't reckon they'll want to argue with.'

Jack and the others left after midnight, and dawn broke as they were approaching the head of the valley. Here they split, Tex heading for the Box S ranch house, while Jack and Brad headed for the vantage point on top of the ridge.

As Tex approached the Box S ranch buildings, a hand standing near the bunkhouse ran over to the ranch house and knocked on the door. Shortly after, Sinclair emerged and stood watching Tex, who rode up to the rancher and stopped. Sinclair looked him over.

'You the owner of this spread?' asked Tex. Sinclair nodded. 'I'm Jed Sinclair,' he said.

'I'm looking for a job,' said Tex. 'I'm a good cowhand, and I know how to use a six-gun. You got any use for a feller like me?'

'Maybe,' replied Sinclair. 'Where are you from?'

'Been punching cows in South Texas,' replied Tex. 'Figured I'd like to look at the range further north. This looks like a pretty good spread you've got here.'

'I'll take you on,' said Sinclair, 'but I'm warning you that you might have to use that gun of yours. Six of my men have been kidnapped over the past week.'

'Well . . .' said Tex, dubiously.

'All my men are getting twice the ordinary rate for a cowhand,' said Sinclair, 'and I'm expecting to get those kidnapped men back real soon.'

'In that case,' said Tex, 'you've got yourself a new hand. My name's Foster, Tex Foster.'

'I ain't got a foreman just now,' said Sinclair, 'so you'll take your orders from me. Take your gear to the bunkhouse over there and find yourself a spare bunk. Then come back and see me.'

'Right,' said Tex. He dismounted, and started leading his horse towards the bunkhouse. Then, suddenly, he turned and shouted to Sinclair who was about to go back into the house.

'You said six of your men were missing?'

'That's right,' replied Sinclair.

'It just struck me,' said Tex, 'that maybe I saw them yesterday.'

'You did,' said Sinclair, showing considerable interest. 'Where was that?'

'It was well south of here,' replied Tex. 'Thirty miles or so. I saw some smoke coming out of a small box canyon, so I got off my horse and sneaked up to the canyon rim to see what was happening inside. There were eight men there and eight horses. Six of the men were tied hand and foot and were sitting against the canyon wall. The other two men were guarding them. Each of the guards was carrying a shotgun. I watched for a while and saw the guards feeding the prisoners. After a while I figured it weren't none of my business, so I left.'

'You're sure there were only two guards?' Sinclair asked him.

'I'm certain of it,' Tex replied.

'Could you tell me what any of the prisoners looked like?' asked Sinclair.

'I reckon so,' said Tex. 'I was fairly close to them.' He started to give a rough description of the men in the guardhouse at the old fort. Sinclair stopped him before he had finished.

'How about the two guards?' he asked. 'What did they look like?'

Tex gave rough descriptions which he knew would mean nothing to Sinclair.

'Those prisoners were my men,' said Sinclair. 'I don't recognize the men guarding them. Can you find that canyon again?'

'Sure,' replied Tex.

Sinclair thought for a moment, then spoke again.

'I don't want to leave the ranch myself,' he said, 'so I'm going to send you and three men to that canyon to free my hands, and bring the two guards

back here with you. Then I can find out who's
behind all this.

'I'm putting my best hand, Dixon, in charge,' he
went on, 'so you'll follow his orders. Be ready to
leave in thirty minutes. I'll expect you all back
tomorrow.'

He walked away to give his orders to Dixon and
the other two hands.

On top of the ridge, Jack and Brad, watching the
Box S buildings, had earlier observed the arrival of
Tex at the ranch house. Then, later, they saw him
leave with three other riders. Jack was disappointed
to see that Sinclair was not in the party. The capture
of the rancher would have to wait. Jack and Brad
ran down the gully to their horses, mounted, and
rode off fast to the south. They were out of sight by
the time Tex and the Box S men had crossed the
ridge.

Once they were out of the valley, Tex led Dixon
and the others southward for about two miles until
they came to a large isolated rock outcrop about
forty feet high, with a roughly square base, thirty feet
by thirty. As Tex, in the lead, came abreast of the
outcrop, and close to it, he stopped and faced the
others, who had come to a halt, three abreast,
behind him. Confounded, the Box S hands stared at
the revolver which had suddenly appeared in Tex's
hand.

'This is as far as we go,' said Tex.

Any thought of resistance on the part of Dixon
and the others was abandoned when Jack and Brad

suddenly appeared from behind the outcrop and ran up, guns in hand, to join Tex.

In half an hour the Box S men had been disarmed, bound, and were being escorted by their captors to the old fort. When they reached it, in the early evening, the three prisoners were put in the cell with the other Box S men, and Jack and his two companions sat down for a meal with Randle and Ranger.

'I think,' said Jack, when they had finished eating, 'that we might have a go at capturing Sinclair now. He's only got three men with him. It shouldn't be too big a job for the three of us, if we plan it right. But we'd better miss out on our sleep tonight, and leave right away, so we can reach the Box S before daybreak. If we leave it too long Sinclair'll start wondering why his men haven't come back.'

They left shortly after and arrived at the Box S an hour and a half before dawn. They rode up to the corral fence, which was some distance from the house, dismounted, and tied their horses to a rail.

'Have a quick look round for guards, will you, Tex?' asked Jack, knowing from past experience that his friend, though a big man, was able to move soundlessly, like a shadow, in the dark.

'And I mean quick, Tex,' Jack went on. 'We ain't got much time before daylight.'

Tex left Jack and Brad and moved soundlessly over to the bunkhouse, all his senses alert. He walked round it, then listened at the door for a moment, before moving on. He passed a large, half-finished shed close to the bunkhouse, and glancing inside he could dimly see a pile of lumber on the floor, obviously intended for use in completing the construction of the building. He circled the barn and cookhouse, then finally the house, listening outside it for a moment, before he returned to Jack and Brad.

'No guards outside the buildings,' he reported, 'and I can't swear to it, but I'm pretty sure there are men sleeping in the bunkhouse.'

'Good,' said Jack. 'We'd better see to the hands in the bunkhouse first. We'll put them out of action, then go for Sinclair. But we could do with a light when we go in to the bunkhouse after the men.'

'Wait outside the bunkhouse and I'll go get a lamp from the cookshack,' said Tex.

He was back in a few minutes with an oil lamp which Jack lit. Holding the lamp, he opened the door of the bunkhouse and stepped quickly inside, drawing his six-gun as he did so. Brad and Tex, also with guns drawn, followed close behind. Jack placed the lamp on a table, then the three intruders stood side by side in the middle of the room, looking at three occupied bunks standing end on to the far wall.

The men lying on the three bunks stirred and sat up, one after the other. Jack recognized one of them as Lassiter, who had been with Bart Sinclair during the attack on the Carson ranch.

'Don't try anything,' he said. There are three guns covering you. Just . . .' He paused as all three

Box S hands slowly rolled off their bunks and lay face down on the floor. It was at that precise moment that Jack suspected that they had fallen into a trap. His suspicion was confirmed when the window on their left was suddenly shattered, and the barrels of two shotguns appeared in the aperture, trained on Jack and his companions. A harsh voice yelled at them from outside.

'Drop those guns, or you're dead!'

Jack and his friends knew that they had no choice in the face of the threat of a load of buckshot at close range. They dropped their guns to the floor.

The door behind them opened and five men came in and checked Jack and his companions for further weapons. The three Box S hands lying on the floor stood up, and the shotgun barrels were withdrawn from the window. A moment later, two more men walked in from outside.

Lassiter was staring at Jack as though he could scarcely believe his eyes.

'It's Silver!' he said.

A big man, who had been the first to enter, ordered Jack and his companions to stand against the wall. He was bearded, with a coarse, brutal face which Jack remembered seeing before on a Wanted poster in his office when he was serving as sheriff.

The man was Grant Morgan, a notorious outlaw wanted for numerous murders and robberies in Texas and New Mexico Territory. The six men with him, all mean-looking characters, must be members of his gang, Jack thought. He wondered how it had come about that Morgan and his gang had suddenly turned up in the valley.

Morgan, pointing to Jack, spoke to Lassiter.

'You called this man Silver,' he said. 'Is he the one that Sinclair was telling us about? The man who was supposed to have died when he was shot on top of the ridge?'

'That's him,' replied Lassiter.

'Do you know the others?' asked Morgan.

'One of them,' replied Lassiter, pointing to Tex. 'He's the one that told Mr Sinclair he knew where the Box S men were being held prisoner.'

'We'd better take the three of them up to the house,' said Morgan. 'Tie their hands behind them.'

Taking Lassiter and one of his men with him, Morgan escorted the prisoners up to the ranch house and knocked hard on the door. After a short while it was opened by Sinclair, with a lighted lamp in his hand. The light fell on the faces of Jack and his companions, standing in front of the two outlaws and Lassiter who were holding guns in their hands.

'We've got three visitors here,' said Morgan, 'and according to Lassiter here, this one in front of me's that dead man Silver you were telling us about. And one of the others is a man you took on yesterday.'

Sinclair stared grimly into Tex's face, then looked closely at Jack.

'You sure,' he asked Lassiter, 'that this is Silver?'

'One hundred per cent sure,' replied the hand.

'So,' said Sinclair, 'both the rancher Bracken and the doctor in Blair were lying.'

He turned to Morgan.

'When I sent word for you to come here and help me out,' he said, 'I never figured you'd get such quick results. Like I told you, this man Silver killed Bart and Clem. And thanks to you, I've got my hands on him at last. He's going to pay for what he done to my boys.'

'After what you told me yesterday when we got here,' said Morgan, 'I guessed that maybe somebody would come after you in the night. So me and my men hid in the back of that half-finished shed near the bunkhouse. And sure enough, these three turned up and went into the bunkhouse after your men. That's when we caught them.'

'Bring them inside,' said Sinclair, 'and let's take a good look at them.'

He led the way into the house and lit a second lamp to give more light. The prisoners were told to stand against one of the walls and Sinclair looked closely at Brad.

'This one I ain't seen before,' he said, then shifted his attention to Tex.

'You had a nerve, Foster, if that's your real name, riding in here and spinning that yarn about leading us to those six hands of mine who disappeared. I'm guessing that the three men who rode out with you have disappeared as well.'

He turned to Morgan.

'It's pretty certain that these men know where nine hands of mine are being held. We've got to get the information out of them.'

'Leave it to us,' said Morgan. 'Seeing as Silver was the one who killed your sons, maybe he's the one we should work on?'

'That's right,' said Sinclair. 'I'm going to enjoy watching this. But take them into the barn first. I don't want this room messed up.'

EIGHT

On the way to the barn, Sinclair called two more of his men out of the bunkhouse to accompany them. Inside the barn he ordered Brad and Tex to sit on the floor with their backs to a wall, while one of his men held a gun on them. Two of Morgan's men then grabbed hold of Jack's arms and held him in a standing position, hard against a wall. His hands were still tied behind him. Morgan walked over and stood in front of him.

'What we want to know, Silver,' he said, 'is exactly where we can find them Box S hands that you're holding. You can tell us right away, or we can find out the hard way.'

Jack looked Morgan straight in the eye, but said nothing.

'All right,' said Morgan, 'if that's the way you want it.'

He drove his right fist twice into the pit of Jack's stomach, and stood back to observe the result. Jack slumped, but was held erect by the two men holding him. Then, punching hard, Morgan attacked Jack's face, hitting him twice on the right jaw and once against his right eye. Blood started to flow from a cut under the right eye. When Morgan paused, breathing heavily, Sinclair moved in and delivered a couple of powerful punches to Jack's ribs and another punch to his face.

Jack appeared to lose consciousness, and the men holding him allowed him to slip down the wall and lie on the floor. Sinclair kicked him hard in the side. Jack's eyes opened as Sinclair was raising his foot to kick him again.

'Stop!' he screamed, cowering back against the wall. 'I'll tell you where they are. They're in a cave—'

He stopped as Tex yelled at him, disgust in his voice. 'Damn you, Jack,' said Tex. 'What about our friends who're on guard there?'

He started rising to his feet to approach Jack, but Morgan rapped him on the head with his gun barrel and he slumped to the floor. Sinclair raised his foot again to kick Jack, who cowered against the wall again, then continued talking.

'They're in a cave,' he said, his voice shaking as if with fear. 'The cave is in a ravine half a mile east of . . .' He stopped as Tex, half-dazed, tried to intervene again, only to sink back to the ground once more under the threat of Morgan's revolver.

Jack continued. 'You have to go to Eagle Mesa, south of here,' he said. 'The ravine is half a mile east of the mesa. The cave is is in the ravine, with its entrance covered by brush.'

'I know Eagle Mesa,' said Morgan. 'We passed it on

the way here. It's about a day's ride south. And we saw some ravines around there. But we didn't ride through any of them.'

'A day's ride, you say,' said Sinclair. 'No wonder we couldn't find it before.'

Contemptuously, he looked down at Jack, still lying on the floor, his face working, and groaning with pain.

'Looks like Silver ain't as tough as I thought,' he said.

He looked out of the window, then spoke to Morgan.

'It's daylight now,' he said. 'You and your men go to that ravine and set my men free and bring them back here.'

'We'll leave after we've eaten,' said Morgan. 'I figure Silver told us the truth, but just in case he didn't, I reckon you should keep these three alive till we get back. I'll leave two of my men here with you. Keep a guard over the prisoners all the time, and at night-time I reckon all the rest of you should stay together in the house.'

'I'll do that,' said Sinclair, 'and I'll expect you back in two or three days. There's some food in the cook-shack. Help yourselves. I sure will be glad when the cook gets back.'

As Morgan walked away, the rancher turned to Lassiter.

'That small shed behind the cookshack,' he said. 'Clear it out. Put the stuff in the barn. Then fix a couple of strong bolts on the outside of the door.

We'll keep Silver and the others in there. Come back here and tell me when you've finished.'

Morgan and four of his men left an hour later, and soon after that Lassiter came to the house, where Sinclair, sitting on a chair with a gun in his hand, was keeping an eye on the prisoners. He and Lasssiter took the three prisoners to the small shed that Lassiter had prepared for them. Jack, bent forward, and walking unsteadily, was prodded on by the barrel of the gun in Sinclair's hand. Inside the shed, the prisoners' feet were tied and their hands were bound together behind their backs. Then Sinclair and Lassiter left, bolting the shed door behind them.

There was silence inside the shed until the sound of voices outside faded away. Then Tex spoke.

'How're you feeling, Jack?' he asked.

'I've often wondered,' replied Jack, 'what it would feel like to be mauled by a bad-tempered grizzly bear. Now I know. But it could have been worse. Maybe I've got a cracked rib or two, and my good looks are going to be spoilt for a while, but I don't think there's anything broken. It's a good thing you chipped in like you did, Tex. Without that, maybe they wouldn't have believed me. As it is, we've gained ourselves a couple of days before Sinclair comes round to the business of getting rid of us. Maybe by that time we can think up some way of getting away from here.

'You feeling all right yourself, Tex, after that pistol-whipping?' Jack went on.

'Sure,' replied Tex. 'I've a bit of a sore head, that's all.'

Jack looked round the shed. There were no windows, but light passing through gaps at the edges of the door faintly illuminated the interior.

'You got any ideas, Jack?' asked Brad, 'about how we might get away from here?'

'Right now, I can't say I have.' replied Jack.

He looked at the rope around his legs and strained on the rope tying his wrists together behind his back. This rope was tied so tightly that his hands could not possibly be used to undo the ropes on either of his two companions, and they were similarly tied. Looking around the bare shed he could see nothing against which a rope could be chafed.

'They've tied us up pretty good,' he said. 'I can't see any of us freeing our hands and feet. We'll just have to wait, and jump on any chance that might come along. Meanwhile, seeing as we had no sleep during the night. I'm going to try and forget all these aches and pains and have a bit of a rest. Maybe we're going to need all our strength later on.'

There was silence in the shed as Jack and his friends, sitting on the floor, leaned back against the wall, closed their eyes and tried to forget that maybe they only had a couple of days left to live.

Food was brought to them at noon by Sinclair and one of Morgan's men. The outlaw untied their wrists so that they could handle their food and drink, while Sinclair held a gun on them. He looked at Jack's bloody and battered features with a grim and cruel satisfaction.

'Don't get the idea,' he said, 'that just because you told us where my men are being held, things are going to be any easier for you.'

'Knowing what a villain you are, Sinclair,' said Tex, 'we didn't get no such idea. You've already murdered Al Jordan and we know you ain't aiming to stop at that. But the law's going to catch up with you in the end.'

Ignoring Tex, Sinclair checked the ropes after Morgan's man had retied the prisoners' hands. Then they left the shed, bolting the door behind them.

The prisoners tried to relax, but for Jack it was difficult. One eye was swollen, and his face ached from the pounding it had received. Also, the area around his stomach and ribs was very painful. After a while he dozed, waking from time to time when the slightest movement of his body caused a fresh spasm of pain.

A further meal was brought to them in the evening just after dark, this time by two of Morgan's men. After they had left the shed, the prisoners could hear occasional movements outside, and now and again they could see the light from the flare of a match. Obviously a guard had been posted outside the shed.

The three prisoners dozed fitfully, and were wakened by the sound of voices outside when the guard was changed at midnight. Just under an hour later, Jack heard a sudden thump against the wall which wakened his two companions. This was followed by the faint sound of movements outside.

Then they heard the sound of the two bolts on the door being withdrawn. A moment later the door opened and a man slipped inside and pulled the door to behind him. He struck a match and peered down at the three prisoners.

'Milt!' whispered Jack and Tex simultaneously, a great sense of relief flooding over them as they recognized their old friend Milt Grayson, ex-deputy sheriff under Jack. Milt produced a knife, and feeling for the ropes in the dark, he freed the hands and feet of the three prisoners. They stood up and flexed their arms and legs.

'The guard, Milt?' asked Jack.

'I had to bend the barrel of my gun over his head,' said Milt. 'He's lying out there, bound and gagged.'

A wave of nausea hit Jack and his legs started to give way, but Brad, standing next to him, felt him sagging, and supported him until he recovered a few minutes later.

'When Milt turned up,' said Jack, 'I thought that maybe we could take Sinclair now. But now I ain't so sure. Drag that guard in here, Milt, then stay outside yourself. I want to look at him, but I don't want him to see your face.'

When Milt had done this, and had gone back outside, Jack struck a match and looked at the guard's face. The man's eyes were open and he looked scared.

'This is one of Sinclair's men,' said Jack. 'Leave him in here and we'll go outside where he can't hear us.'

They left the shed, bolted it, and moved away a short distance. Milt joined them, and Jack told him about the arrival of the Morgan gang on the scene.

'According to what Morgan suggested to Sinclair before we were put in the shed,' said Jack, 'there'll be Sinclair himself in the house, with two of his own men and two outlaws that Morgan left behind. And those last two are certain to be experienced gunslingers. What's more, I ain't exactly fighting fit myself. So I don't think this is a good time for us to try and capture Sinclair. What we'd better do is find our horses and leave before somebody comes out to relieve the guard.'

'I know where to find the horses and some tack,' said Tex. 'Come with me, Milt, and lend a hand.'

'We'll wait behind the barn,' said Jack. He was still feeling a little faint, and the pain around his ribs was bothering him.

Twenty minutes later Tex and Milt returned with four saddled horses, including the one on which Milt had arrived.

'Milt,' said Jack. 'I want you to go to Bridger and keep an eye on the Carsons. Did anybody in town see you visit the store?'

'No,' replied Milt, 'I got in after dark and Mr Carson told me exactly what's been happening here. And he said that the saloon keeper, who's a friend of his, had told him that he'd overheard Lassiter and another Box S hand talking in the saloon during the day. From what he heard he was pretty sure that you three were being held at the

Box S. That's how I come to be here.'

'Lucky for us you turned up when you did,' said Jack. 'Like I said, I'd like you to go to Bridger and keep an eye on the Carsons for me. But don't let anybody outside the Drurys and Carsons know that we're working together.'

'Right,' said Milt. 'Where will you three go?'

'To the old fort where we're holding the Box S hands,' replied Jack, and told Milt exactly where the fort was located.

'We've got to see that everything's all right there,' he went on, 'and we've got to work out some way of dealing with the Morgan gang, now they've turned up. We'll get in touch with you soon.'

They parted, Milt heading east for Bridger, Jack and the others west for the fort. The long ride, at a time when his body badly needed rest, was torture for Jack, and he was just about all in when they arrived at the fort a little after daybreak.

Randle and Ranger had nothing unusual to report, but pointed out that food stocks were getting low. Jack asked them to ride to a small town which Tex remembered riding through, about ten miles west of the fort. There they would be able buy a good supply of provisions to replenish their stocks.

Jack then washed the congealed blood from his face and after eating a little food he went inside the guardhouse to lie down and ease his aching body.

While Jack and the others were resting, Morgan and his men were painstakingly searching the area around Eagle Mesa for men imprisoned in a cave in a ravine. When, eventually, they realized that they had been duped, Morgan exploded with rage, and after only a few hours' rest he and his men headed back towards the Box S, with Morgan vowing to make Jack and the others pay heavily for his wasted journey.

When he eventually reached the Box S he was incensed at the news of the prisoners' escape.

'You got any idea who it was who freed them?' he asked, angrily.

'No,' replied Sinclair. 'It was dark. One of my hands was on guard, but he was hit from behind. He never saw the face of the man who did it.'

'My guess is,' said Morgan, 'that Silver and the others have gone to the place where your men are being held. And we still ain't got no idea just where that place is. I reckon you've been too easy on these people up to now, Sinclair. If you give me a free hand maybe I can get some results.'

'That's what I'm paying you for,' said Sinclair. 'Go ahead.'

'Right,' said Morgan. 'I'm taking all my men with me to pay Carson a visit at the store in Bridger.'

In Bridger, at around one in the afternoon, the Drurys and Carsons, together with Milt, had just finished a meal. Glancing out of the window, Milt saw seven men walking their horses round to the back of the store. The storekeeper and Carson saw them at the same time.

'Morgan and his men for sure,' said Milt.

Drury rose and rushed Milt through into the store. He took an old tattered shirt from a hook on the wall and handed it to Milt.

'Put this on quick,' he said, then handed him an apron to wear and put a large broom in his hands.

'My gun said Milt. 'When I sat down to eat I took my gunbelt off, and Mrs Drury took it away somewhere.'

'I'll get it for you,' said Drury. 'In the meantime, you'd best start sweeping. It's lucky none of those men outside knows who you are or why you're here.'

Drury returned to his wife and the Carsons in the living-room, but before he could ask his wife where Milt's gun was, Morgan and two of his men walked in. They had come in through the rear door without knocking. Each of them had a gun in his hand.

'Search the place,' said Morgan.

Drury started to protest, but Morgan held a gun on him and told him to shut his mouth.

Morgan's men searched the living area of the building, then walked into the store. Milt, busy sweeping the floor, paused as the men came in, guns in hand. They glanced at him, then walked around the store and came back to him. Milt looked scared.

'Can I get you something?' he asked, his voice shaking a little.

The two men ignored him and returned to Morgan in the living-room, closing the door behind them.

'No sign of Silver and the others,' they said.

Milt walked up to the door which led to the living-room and opened it just a fraction, so that he could hear what was going on inside the room. Carson, who was close to the door, noticed that it was slightly ajar.

Milt realized that, even if he had a weapon, any move he made, single-handed, against the seven outlaws would be doomed to failure, and could result in the deaths of innocent people.

Morgan looked at the Carsons and the Drurys.

'Which of you is Carson?' he asked.

'That's me,' said Carson.

'Me and my men,' said Morgan, 'have been hired by Sinclair of the Box S to move you and your family out of the valley and to get rid of Silver and his friends. But first we have to free the Box S hands that Silver's holding somewhere.

'And that's where you come in, Carson,' he went on. 'I figure you're bound to know where those missing hands are. And you're going to tell me where that place is, right now.'

He held up his hand as Carson attempted to speak, and continued.

'If you don't, we're going to take your daughter away right now, and I can promise you, Carson, you'll never see her again. If she stays alive, you won't know what hell she's going through. If she does die, you'll never know when and where it happened.

'If you *do* tell us where the Box S men are,' Morgan continued, 'we'll take you and your daughter to the Box S and you'll be held there until my men have freed them and have taken Silver and the others prisoner. If we find you've lied to us, *you'll* be killed and your daughter will disappear, like I told you before.'

There was silence for a while when Morgan stopped speaking. Agonized, Carson looked at his daughter. Mary looked as if she was about to speak.

'Leave Carson here,' said Morgan to one of his men, 'and take the others into the other room.'

While the Drurys and Carson's wife and daughter were being moved out Carson took a decision. He was sure that Milt had been listening to his conversation with Morgan. He decided that the risk of duping Morgan once again was justified.

'Right,' said Morgan, when he and Carson were alone. 'Now we can have a quiet talk. You ain't got no choice, Carson, if you don't want your girl to suffer.'

'You ain't got no right to do this, Morgan,' said Carson, angrily, 'but Mary comes first with me. I guess you know that. I'll have to tell you where the Box S men are. But I want your guarantee that when you find them there, Mary and me are going to be freed.'

Even as he spoke he knew that any such guarantee would be worthless.

'You have my word on that,' said Morgan.

Carson then described a place sixty miles north of the valley which he knew well, having spent some time in the area four years ago, when he was looking round for a good location for his ranch. He told Morgan to watch out for Buffalo Rock, a massive outcrop which stood alone and was visible for miles around. A little over a mile to the north of the outcrop was a deep, winding gorge. Somewhere in this gorge, said Sinclair, the Box S prisoners were being held.

'You can go out now, Carson,' said Morgan, 'and get horses for you and your daughter. And if anybody asks, you're riding out with us for a friendly talk with Sinclair. Say anything else, and your daughter'll suffer.'

Carson was back in twenty minutes with two horses. He waited outside. As Morgan was leaving the house with Mary, he spoke to her mother and the Drurys.

'Say anything around town about this that causes trouble for us,' he said, 'and Carson and the girl will suffer, and this store will burn down. And the same applies if anybody goes out to the Box S and tries to free them.'

As the outlaws rode off with Carson and Mary, Milt came out of the store and, standing at the window with Carson's wife and the Drurys, he watched them leave. When they had ridden out of sight, he told the others about the conversation he had heard between Carson and Morgan when they were alone in the living-room.

'Those outlaws are riding off with Mr Carson and his daughter,' he said, bitterly, 'and there weren't a darned thing I could do to stop them.'

'There was nothing you *could* do,' said Ellen Carson, her face white and strained. 'But what can we do now to help them? They'll be in real trouble when Morgan finds he's been tricked again.'

'I'm going to ride out straight away to the fort to let Jack and the others know what's happened here,' said Milt.

NINE

Milt arrived at the fort around ten in the evening. On the way he had stopped at the point on the ridge previously used by Jack, which overlooked the Box S buildings. From this vantage point, south of the ranch, he saw Morgan and his six men assemble outside the ranch house, then ride off to the north.

Milt told Jack and the others of the kidnapping of Carson and his daughter, and of Morgan's departure on a second wild-goose chase. Jack, feeling a lot better after a rest, considered this latest move on Morgan's part with mounting concern. Carson and his daughter *must* be freed.

He turned to Milt.

'You said, Milt, that all Morgan's men rode off with him?'

'That's right,' said Milt.

'That leaves Sinclair on the Box S with three of his hands and Carson and Mary. We've *got* to capture Sinclair and free the Carsons, and we must do it before Morgan and his men get back. I reckon that if

104

we want to do the job quickly, without the Carsons getting hurt, all six of us should ride to the Box S right now, if that's all right with Josh and Hank.'

'Count me in,' said Randle.

'Me too,' said Ranger, 'but what about the prisoners?'

'The cell is too strong for them to break out of,' said Jack. 'We'll leave enough food and water in the cell to last them for a while, and we'll come back here as soon as we've captured Sinclair, before we take him to the law. Better get moving right away. We *must* get there before daylight so's we can get up to the ranch buildings without being seen.'

They made a hurried departure, taking two extra saddled horses with them, and rode as fast as they were able. It was a clear night, and they arrived at a point a quarter of a mile clear of the Box S buildings, with well over an hour to go before dawn.

'Tex,' said Jack. 'Go ahead on foot and have a good look round, will you? But make sure they don't see you.'

Tex dismounted and vanished into the night. Twenty minutes later he materialized out of the darkness and walked up to Jack.

'There's nobody in any of the outbuildings,' he said. 'I figure they're all inside the house, prisoners as well. I heard some sounds from the ground floor and there's a dim light coming from in there, but I couldn't see inside. My guess is that the hands are in there acting as guards, with Sinclair and the Carsons upstairs in the bedrooms. There are two windows high up at the back of the house. I reckon they belong to two bedrooms.'

'When you looked in the barn, Tex,' asked Jack. 'Did you notice whether there was a ladder there?'

'Yes, there was,' replied Tex, 'leading up to the hayloft.'

'Good,' said Jack, and spent a few minutes discussing his plan of action with the others. Then they tied their horses to the corral rails.

Josh and Hank, armed with rifles, took up positions under cover, facing the front of the house.

'When we want you to start shooting,' said Jack as he left them, 'I'll strike a match from somewhere in your view at one of the back corners of the house. And when we want you to stop, one of us'll shout "Stop, Josh!" While you're firing, keep up a steady fire and send your bullets into the front wall of the house, but not through the windows. You've got plenty of ammunition.'

Tex, with the others close behind him, led the way to the barn. They went inside and Jack lit a match for a brief instant, while he inspected a ladder resting against the edge of an aperture in the floor of the hayloft above.

'That'll do,' he said, and taking hold of the ladder, the others followed Tex as he circled the house, too far away from it to be spotted in the dark by anyone inside. They approached the house from the rear, and laying the ladder on the ground they took cover behind a buckboard standing about ten yards from the house.

Jack ran to a back corner of the house and lit a match. After it had flared he quickly extinguished it and ran back to the others. The first shot came from Josh, just as Jack sank down behind the buckboard. A little later Hank fired, and he and Josh continued to fire alternately. Jack and the others heard what sounded like return fire from the house.

At the same time, a light showed in one of the bedrooms for a moment, before being extinguished. Then the watchers saw dimly, in the darkness, that one of the two windows was being opened. A moment later someone poked a head out of the window and looked around briefly before the head was withdrawn and the window pulled to.

Jack was sure that the head had belonged to Sinclair. He waited a few minutes, then he and Tex carried the ladder over and placed it under the window that had been opened. Jack climbed up the ladder and slowly pulled the window open. It had not been properly fastened inside. Holding his gun in his hand he looked into the darkness of the room. There was no indication of any movement inside.

He climbed through the window and struck a match. The room was empty. He called softly to his friends below to climb up into the room, then led the way to the passage outside the door and along to the door of the second bedroom. There was continuous gunfire now from down below. Outside, dawn was beginning to break.

Jack felt for the door handle and turned it, but the door refused to open. Near the handle he felt a key in the lock. When he turned this the door opened, and he and his companions slipped inside and closed the door behind them. They could hear movement inside the room. Jack struck a match and lit an oil lamp standing on a bedside table. He turned it down low. Then he and the others looked around.

There were two beds in the room. Mary was sitting up in one of them, staring at the four men who had entered. Her father, propped up on one elbow, recognized the one closest to him as Tex and breathed a great sigh of relief. Then, as Mary recognized Jack she jumped out of the bed and ran into his arms. He could feel her trembling.

'It's all right, Mary,' he said, 'we've come to get you away from here and to capture Sinclair at the same time. That gunfire you hear outside is coming from Hank and Josh. Both of you get dressed as quick as you can.'

When Mary and her father were ready to leave, Jack led them into the next bedroom and showed them the ladder outside the window. He told them to climb down it and hide behind the buckboard outside until he came for them later.

Carson climbed down first, then Jack helped Mary out on to the ladder.

'You'll be coming for us soon?' she asked, as she started to climb down.

'Pretty soon,' Jack replied. 'It shouldn't take us long to deal with those men downstairs.'

Jack turned and left the room, with the others close behind him. He moved slowly along the passage to the head of the stairs, then down the stairs to the door at the bottom which led to the living-room. The door was slightly ajar.

From the room behind it they could hear the sound of the bullets from Hank and Josh striking the wall of the house, and the sound of return fire from inside. Looking through the narrow gap at the edge of the door Jack could not see the occupants of the room, who were outside his field of vision, but he could see that there was now sufficient light coming into the room from outside to suit his purpose.

Quietly, he whispered to the others, then pushed the door open. With guns drawn, the four stepped quickly into the room and stood facing the two windows against which, two at each window, Sinclair and his men were standing, peering outwards. All four were holding rifles.

A bullet from Hank or Josh hit the wall outside and two of the Box S men fired their rifles in reply. In the ensuing silence Jack called out to Sinclair and his men.

'There are four guns on you men,' he shouted. 'Put your rifles down.'

All four men tensed. Then Sinclair and two of his men started to lower their rifles to the floor. But the fourth man, Lassiter, who was holding his rifle to his shoulder when Jack called out, started to swing round to fire at the intruders, but was thwarted when a bullet from Jack's Peacemaker smashed into the butt of his rifle and jerked it out of his hands.

After Sinclair and the other two hands had laid

down their rifles, Jack ordered the rancher and his men to turn and face him. Tex went to the window and called to Josh and Hank to stop firing. Then, while Jack and Brad held guns on them, Tex took the revolvers from Sinclair and his men and checked them for other weapons. While he was doing this Hank and Josh came in.

Almost apoplectic with rage, Sinclair glared at Jack and his companions.

'You won't get away with this, Silver,' he said. 'Morgan and his gang'll see to that when he gets back.'

'It may be a while before they turn up,' said Jack. 'They ain't going to find it as easy as they thought to locate those missing men of yours. I reckon you and I will be long gone before they get back. We'll be well on our way to the US marshal in Amarillo.'

They tied the three hands in such a way that though they would be able to free themselves, this would take some time. Then, leaving Tex to guard Sinclair and his men, Jack went outside to Mary and her father. Mary was lying flat on the ground behind the buckboard. Her father was kneeling beside her. He looked up as Jack approached.

'Mary's been hurt?' asked Jack, concerned.

'Yes,' replied Carson, 'and I'm worried about her. When she was halfway down the ladder her foot slipped and she fell the rest of the way. When she hit the ground she fell over, and hit her head pretty hard. She's got a bad bruise on the forehead and she's unconscious. I just can't bring her round.'

Jack knelt down beside Mary and had a good look at the bruise. She had obviously suffered a fairly heavy blow. He spoke to Carson.

'We've captured Sinclair and his men,' he said, 'and we'll be leaving here soon. We've got to get Mary to a doctor, so I reckon we should take her to Doc Gannon in Blair. He's a friend of mine. We'll take her on this buckboard. I'll get a mattress and some blankets from the house. You stay out here with Mary while I get things organized.'

Jack walked back into the house and called the others over to him, leaving Sinclair and his men out of earshot. He told them about Mary's fall and of his decision to take her to see Doc Gannon.

'We could all go to my ranch house,' said Brad. 'It ain't far out of town. Then we could get the doctor to come out and see Mary.'

'That's a good idea,' said Jack. 'We'll do that. Now, about the prisoners at the fort,' he went on. 'Even though we've got Sinclair now, I reckon we should hold on to the prisoners at the fort because the law might want words with them. So as soon as we're ready to take Sinclair to Amarillo, I'd like Milt to ride to the fort with Josh and Hank to look after the prisoners.'

Jack asked Josh and Hank to saddle a horse for Sinclair and to find and saddle the horses Carson and Mary had ridden on from Bridger to the Box S. He also asked them to hitch a couple of horses to the buckboard. Then he walked over to Sinclair, and ordered him to walk outside with him, leaving the Box S hands inside the house.

'You've got some riding to do, Sinclair,' he said. 'Seeing as there's no law around here to come to *you* and stop you from riding roughshod over everybody in the valley, we're going to take *you* to the law instead. There's a US marshal in Amarillo who's going to be very interested to hear about the murder of Brad Jordan's brother and the rustling of his horse herd. And there's also the matter of you taking over the Carson ranch house and kidnapping Mr Carson and his daughter.

'And just to give the US marshal proof of all this,' Jack continued, 'we're taking plenty of witnesses along with us.'

Although Sinclair didn't speak, his look was murderous as Brad tied his hands and led him over to the horse which Josh had just brought for him.

Shortly after this, as the buckboard pulled up outside the house, one of the hands they were leaving behind caught a glimpse through the half-open door of Mary, lying unconscious on the floor of the buckboard, with her father sitting beside her. Five minutes later Jack and the others left the Box S with Sinclair as prisoner.

Halfway to Brad's ranch, Carson called out to Jack, who was driving the buckboard.

'Mary's coming round,' he said.

Jack stopped the buckboard and stepped into the back. Mary, lying on a mattress, looked up at him. Her father was explaining to her what had happened.

'Yes, I remember falling,' she said, and her hand

went up to the angry bruise on her forehead. Then she tried to sit up, but sank back with a cry of pain as she moved her leg.

'My ankle!' she said.

Jack bent down to look at it. It was badly swollen.

'It's been damaged in the fall,' he said. 'I'll fasten my bandanna round it to try and hold it steady. Keep your leg as still as you can. How's your head feeling?'

'I can think straight,' she said, 'but I've got a bad headache.'

'We'll get a doctor to you as soon as we can,' said Jack.

When Morgan and his men reached Buffalo Rock they slept until daybreak, then rode north for a further mile and found what looked like the deep, winding gorge that Carson had described. But after exploring every nook and cranny of it, then searching the surrounding country for a radius of five miles without finding any sign of the missing Box S hands by the end of the day, Morgan realized that he had been tricked again. He was almost beside himself with rage, and suspecting that Jack may have made an attempt to rescue the Carsons, he decided that he and his men would have a meal, then ride back to the Box S through the night.

They were halfway through the meal, seated round the camp-fire, when they heard a call, and a mounted man rode into the circle of light around the fire. Both his hands were raised in the air. He stopped in front of Morgan.

'Howdy, Grant,' he said.

Surprised, Morgan recognized the rider as an outlaw, Brett Spencer, a distant cousin, who had ridden with him several times in the past, but who mainly worked on his own. He had not seen Spencer for some time and wondered what he was doing in those parts.

'Brett,' he said. 'There's some coffee here, and grub if you want it.'

Spencer dismounted and led his horse to the picket line. Then he sat down next to Morgan. He was handed a mug of coffee and some food.

'I've been on a visit to Pueblo, Colorado, ' he said, 'and I'm on my way back to Fort Worth, Texas. I spotted your camp-fire and sneaked up to see who you were. I was mighty surprised to recognize you and the boys.' He did not enlarge on the purpose of his trip, but asked Morgan how he came to be in the area.

Morgan told him how he had been hired by Sinclair and explained that he was searching for nine Box S hands who were being held prisoner somewhere in the area.

'Being held prisoner?' said Spencer, thoughtfully. 'I wonder . . .' His voice tailed off.

'Wonder what?' asked Morgan, sharply.

'It's something that happened just over a week ago,' replied Spencer, 'when I was heading for Pueblo. I was riding through New Mexico Territory, not far from the Texas border, roughly southwest of here. It was after dark and I was looking for a place to camp for the night when I came on the remains of an old Army fort with just one building still standing.

'I could see there were lights inside the building,' he went on, 'and I was mighty curious about who was in there. I got off my horse and sneaked up to the building. When I got close I could see it was the old guardhouse. Two of the windows were barred and I could hear voices behind them. I risked a look through one of the windows and saw that the cell door was closed. Four men were standing with their backs to me and I'm sure there were others lying on their bunks out of sight.

'I listened outside another window that wasn't barred,' he continued, 'and I heard voices inside. I figured they must be lawmen, holding prisoners in the guardhouse for the night, so I didn't waste no time getting away from there. But maybe those are the men you're looking for.'

'There's a good chance they are,' said Morgan, 'and *if* they are, it's likely Silver and the others are there as well. We'll ride there right now. You got time to lead us to the place, Brett?'

'Sure,' said Spencer. 'but I'll have to leave you as soon as we get there. I've got urgent business in Fort Worth.'

Riding in a south-westerly direction they reached the old fort before noon the following day. They approached it with caution, then observed it for some time from a distance. No movement in and out of the guardhouse was observed. Eventually, they rode up to the guardhouse, encountering no opposition on the way, and found the Box S prisoners in the cell. They released the prisoners, had a few hours' sleep, then headed for the Box S.

TEN

When they reached the Jordan ranch Jack and the
others found that Brad's brother Jesse had arrived
there, in response to Brad's telegraph message. Brad
introduced him to the others, then Jack rode off
towards Blair after he had carried Mary into the
house.

Brad told Jesse of the events which had taken
place since he had sent the telegram, then they went
over to the barn, where Sinclair had been tied to a
post by Tex and Hank. They stood in front of him.

'This is the man,' said Brad, 'who murdered our
brother Al out by the corral and stole our horses.'

Sinclair paled as the brothers regarded him with a
look of concentrated fury.

'Why don't we string him up right now?' asked Jesse.

'No,' said Brad. 'That's how I felt at first, but I
reckon it's a job for the law.'

'You going to keep him here in the barn?' asked
Jesse.

'I reckon so,' replied Brad, 'for the time being
anyhow. We'll keep him tied to that post, and some

117

of us'll be sleeping in here, so we can watch him during the night.'

Jack found Doc Gannon at home. He recognized Jack as soon as he opened the door.

'You're supposed to be dead,' he said, smiling.

'Can't think how that story got around,' grinned Jack. 'Thanks for helping me like you did. Could you come with me to Brad Jordan's place? There's a lady there who had a bad fall. She hit her head hard and damaged her ankle.'

'I'll go there with you right away,' said Gannon.

On the ride to the Jordan ranch Jack told the doctor of the events which had taken place since they had last met.

'You ain't exactly been leading a quiet life, have you?' observed Gannon. 'I sure hope you manage to get Sinclair to Amarillo before Morgan catches up with you.'

'We could've done that easy if Mary hadn't had that fall,' said Jack, 'but it looks like we may have to hang around here for a while with Sinclair, till she's ready to travel. We can't leave her behind, not with Morgan around.'

When they reached the Jordan ranch Jack took the doctor inside to see Mary. On the way in, he introduced him to the others. Mary was lying on a bed in a small room downstairs. Jack and Carson went in with Gannon.

The doctor looked at Mary's head wound and asked about her headache. Then he closely examined her ankle.

'There's one good thing about the ankle,' he said, when he had finished. 'It ain't fractured and it ain't dislocated. I'm pretty sure it's just a sprain. I'm going to bandage it up well, to stop any movement in the joint. And for the time being, young lady, you mustn't put any weight on it.

'As for the bang on the head,' he went on, 'we've got to hope that it didn't do any damage inside there. It must have been quite a blow to knock you out like that. You've *got* to stay in bed till that headache goes and you're free from dizzy spells. I'll ride out again tomorrow to see how you're coming on.'

Jack spoke to Gannon as he was about to ride off.

'We'd appreciate it, Doc,' he said, 'If you wouldn't mention to anybody that we're here. Just in case Morgan got to hear about it.'

'You can rely on that,' Gannon assured him.

Over the next two days Mary's ankle gradually improved, but she was still suffering from a headache and the doctor insisted that she must continue resting in bed.

On the evening of the second day, Jack, who by now had almost fully recovered from the beating he had received, decided to ride over to Bridger for news of the movements of Morgan and his gang. It was late in the evening when he walked up to the rear of the store, having first made sure that the building was not under observation. Drury answered his knock and let him in.

He told Mary's mother and the Drurys that they were holding Sinclair until Mary recovered from a fall, then they would take him to the law in Amarillo.

Drury told Jack that the Morgan gang and the missing Box S hands had turned up the previous day. He said that the news was all over town about Sinclair's disappearance and about Morgan finding the missing Box S hands over the border in New Mexico Territory. Also, one of the Box S hands had been heard to say in the saloon that he had seen Mary lying in a buckboard, badly hurt, at the time that Sinclair was captured.

Drury went on to say that several copies of a hand-written poster had appeared on buildings in town that evening offering a $1,000 reward for information concerning the whereabouts of Jed Sinclair and the men who had kidnapped him. The poster mentioned that the kidnappers may be accompanied by an injured woman travelling on a buckboard.

Jack, disturbed by the news that Morgan now had a total of fifteen men at his disposal, wondered how the outlaw had managed to find out where the Box S men were being held prisoner. It was also, he thought, unfortunate that Morgan was aware of Mary's condition. The outlaw would reason that this might delay the handover of Sinclair to the law, and would probably lead to an intensive search in the area for Jack and the others, as well as a close watch on all the possible routes to Amarillo.

After assuring Ellen Carson that her husband was well and that Mary was recovering from her injury, Jack took his leave of her and the Drurys and rode back to the Jordan ranch. It was after midnight when he arrived, but all the men were still up, awaiting his return. He told Carson that his wife was well, then repeated to them all that Drury had told him about Morgan and the release of the Box S hands from the fort. Then he asked Carson how Mary was feeling.

'The ankle's a mite easier,' he replied, 'but I'm worried about her head. That headache she had ain't improved any.'

'We mustn't let Mary think we're worried about having to stay on here because of her,' said Jack. 'That wouldn't do her any good at all. Let's see what Doc Gannon says next time he comes.

'What it all boils down to is this,' he continued. 'Morgan will be aiming to free Sinclair before we get him to Amarillo. He'll be watching the trails to the north and he'll be searching the area for us, and for a doctor who's treated an injured woman recently. I've spoken to Gannon about this and I'm sure he'll say nothing about seeing Mary.

'We can't move Mary just now,' he went on, 'so if Morgan's men find us here, we'll have a fight on our hands, which is the last thing we want just now. But maybe we can lay a false trail to keep them occupied for a while. That is, if Jesse here is willing to help us out. He's the only one of us who's never been seen by the men at the Box S. And I don't think it's likely he'll come to any harm if he does what I have in mind.'

'I'll do anything I can,' said Jesse. 'Anything that'll help us to hand Sinclair over to the law.'

'Right,' said Jack, and went on to give the details of

his plan to the others. Then he took a sheet of writing paper which Brad found for him. He spent some time writing on the paper, then showed it to the others before finally handing it to Jesse.

'Dirty it up and crease it a bit, Jesse,' he said, 'so it looks like it's been in your pocket for a while. I've been figuring,' he went on, 'that nobody in Bridger knows you. Is that so?'

'That's right,' replied Jesse, 'I've never been there. In fact I've never been in this area before.'

'Good,' said Jack, and they all prepared to turn in.

Carson went in to check on Mary and came out almost immediately to ask Jack if he would go in to see her.

She was sitting up in bed. Her face was pale and strained. Jack asked her how she was feeling.

'A little dizzy now and again,' she said, 'and I wish this headache would go away. But my ankle feels a lot better. I'm hoping the doctor'll say I'm fit to ride the next time he comes.'

'I don't think so,' said Jack. 'You just rest easy, and as soon as as you're feeling better we'll be on our way.'

'I'm worried,' she said, 'because I'm holding you up. Maybe you could leave me here with Jesse while you and the others take Sinclair to Amarillo. I know that you and father and Brad have to go along, to testify about Sinclair's crimes.'

'We can't do that, Mary,' said Jack. 'Morgan's already captured you once. We can't risk that happening again. We'll all go to Amarillo together.

We're working on a plan now to keep Morgan and the others occupied for a spell while you rest up a bit longer.'

Jesse left the following morning, an hour before daybreak, and headed for Bridger. On the way into town he stopped to read the notice, tacked to the wall of the barber's shop, offering the $1,000 reward for information concerning Sinclair's whereabouts. He pulled away one of a bundle of spare copies tacked to the wall, then left town and headed for the Box S ranch.

As he was approaching the ranch buildings he could see some activity around the ranch house. A dozen mounted men were waiting outside it. As he rode up to the house the door opened and a man stepped out. From Jack's description Jesse knew that this was Morgan. He stopped in front of the outlaw.

'What d'you want?' asked Morgan.

Jesse took the poster out of his pocket and showed it to the outlaw. 'Maybe I can help you to find this Sinclair,' he said.

'Come inside,' said Morgan, and beckoned Lassiter and his *segundo*, a man called Rafferty, to accompany them. In the living-room he told Jack to say his piece.

'My name's Ryan,' said Jesse. 'I'm riding back from Colorado to San Antonio. I helped drive a trail herd up there earlier in the year.

'I picked up this poster in Bridger this morning,' he went on, 'and I'm sure I've seen the folks and the buckboard that's mentioned in it.'

'When and where?' asked Morgan.

'About fifty miles north~west of here,' replied Jesse, 'riding north along the New Mexico border. They were about four miles north of a small town called Latigo. And the time was yesterday morning. I passed close by them and saw a girl lying on the buckboard. It was moving pretty slow. There were six men all told, and one of them looked like his hands were tied.'

'Describe him,' said Morgan.

Jesse gave the outlaw a passable description of Sinclair.

'You got any proof,' asked Morgan, 'that you're who you say you are?'

Jesse looked surprised. 'I guess not,' he replied. 'You need proof?'

'Let's say,' growled Morgan, sourly, 'that I'm tired of going off on wild-goose chases.'

'Well, I'm sorry,' said Jesse, 'I ain't . . .' He broke off, then continued. 'I've just remembered. This letter's good enough proof, I reckon.'

He pulled a folded sheet of paper out of his vest pocket and handed it to Morgan. The outlaw studied it closely. It was addressed to Buck Jardine, Lazy J Ranch, Texas. It read: 'Bob Ryan, who brings you this letter, is a good trail hand. If you need a cowhand on the ranch I reckon he'd do a good job. Rufe Pryor, Trail Boss.'

Morgan handed the letter back to Jesse.

'When do I get the money?' asked Jesse.

'When we get Sinclair,' replied the outlaw. 'You coming along with us?'

'Can't do that,' replied Jesse. 'I've got to get to San Antonio as soon as I can. You can send the money to me there. I'll give you an address.'

Morgan hesitated for a moment. Then he agreed, and Jesse wrote down an address in San Antonio to which he said the money could be sent. Then he left and headed for Bridger and the Jordan ranch.

In the Box S ranch house Morgan discussed their next move with Rafferty and Lassiter.

'I know that town Latigo that Ryan was talking about,' said Lassiter. 'There's some mighty rough country north of there. If Silver and the others are hiding out somewhere, they could be hard to find.'

'They were moving when Ryan saw them,' said Morgan. 'I reckon they're heading for Amarillo, like Silver said they were going to do. But they can't travel fast with a buckboard. I reckon we can catch up with them long before they get anywhere near to Amarillo.

'Better leave a couple of men here to look after things,' he went on. 'The rest of us will go after Silver and the others.'

They left fifteen minutes later, heading north-west.

As Jesse was passing through Bridger on his way back to the Jordan ranch, he saw a knot of people standing outside the store. He dismounted and spoke to a man on the fringe of the group.

'Something wrong in there?' he asked.

'It's George Drury, the storekeeper,' said the man. 'He's dead. Seems like he stayed up last night after

Emily had gone to bed. She fell asleep and when she woke later on there was no sign of George in the house. He was missing until somebody found him about half an hour ago in an old deserted shack on the edge of town. Seems like he'd been beaten up so bad that it killed him. Nobody knows who done it, but two men from that Morgan gang were seen leaving town well after midnight.'

Jesse knew that Carson and the storekeeper were related, and that Carson and Mary had been staying at the store when Morgan kidnapped them. Saddened by the news he rode back to the Jordan ranch and told Jack and the other men of Drury's death.

'It was Morgan's doing, for sure,' said Jack, seething with anger. 'He was trying to find out from Drury where we were. And Drury didn't actually know. I didn't mention our whereabouts when I saw him yesterday, and he didn't ask.'

'Poor Emily,' said Carson angrily. 'Morgan has got to pay for this.'

Jack turned to Jesse, who told him that Morgan had taken the bait. The news of the outlaw's departure on another fool's errand came as a huge relief to the others.

'I was feeling worried about my wife,' said Carson, 'alone in the store with Emily, although I can't imagine even Morgan attacking a couple of defenceless women right in the middle of town. But they should be safe for a while now. And my wife will be a comfort and a help to Emily.'

'This gives us a breathing-space,' said Jack, 'and hopefully enough time to get Mary fit again while Morgan's away.'

The doctor came out later in the day and examined Mary. Jack spoke to him as he came out of the house. He asked how the patient was coming on.

'The ankle's doing fine,' said Gannon. 'I reckon she could ride with it if we bandaged it up pretty tight. But she still has the headache and I'm worried that maybe her brain has been injured. She *must* carry on resting for now. I'll be out again tomorrow morning to see her.'

When the doctor had departed Jack went and sat with Mary for a while. He told her about Jesse's visit to the Box S and said there was no danger of a visit by Morgan and his men for the time being. He didn't mention the news of Drury's death, knowing that her father was keeping it from her until she was feeling better.

The following morning, when Jack went in to see Mary, the change in her was remarkable. The strained look had gone from her face and she smiled at him as he came into the room.

'The headache's completely gone,' she said. 'It went during the night, and there's no dizziness now. I'm sure I'm fit to travel.'

'That's great news,' said Jack. 'Let's see what the doctor says when he gets here.'

Gannon turned up an hour later. When he had examined Mary he had a word with her father and Jack.

'I know how important it is for you to get moving,' he said. 'I reckon Mary's fit to ride now, but you'll have to lift her on and off her horse. That ankle still needs more rest, so don't let her put any weight on it for a while. And don't ride too fast.'

They thanked the doctor, and when he had ridden off Jack told the others that they would be setting off for Amarillo with Sinclair, after a noon meal. They would circle round the east end of the valley so as to avoid any danger of meeting up with Morgan and his men.

After an uneventful ride they reached Amarillo three days later with their prisoner. First they stopped at an hotel in the centre of town, and Jack carried Mary up to a room. Then he rejoined the others and they sought out the office of the US marshal, Drew Baxter. When they reached it they found Baxter inside, alone. His eyebrows lifted as Jack walked in, followed by Sinclair, with his hands tied, Milt, Tex and Brad. The others stayed outside.

Jack introduced himself and his companions. Then he told Baxter that he had brought Sinclair in for arrest on charges of murder, horse-stealing and kidnapping, and that he and the men with him would bear witness to these crimes. He went on to describe the encounters with Sinclair, Morgan and their men since he had first arrived in Bridger.

The marshal, a tall, thin, middle-aged man with sparse hair and a moustache which drooped past the corners of his mouth, listened with considerable interest. He spoke when Jack had finished.

'You wouldn't be the Jack Silver who served as a county sheriff in South Texas, would you?' he asked.

'The same,' Jack replied. 'I quit a couple of months ago.'

'I was a lawman in Fort Worth for a spell,' said Baxter, 'and I heard a lot about the good work you were doing down there.

'I'm going to slap Sinclair into a cell,' he went on, 'then I'll take your statements about the crimes he's committed. Judge Trasker'll be here in a week's time to try the case. I'd be obliged if you'd all stay here for the trial. Meantime, just stay where you are for a minute.'

He took Sinclair through a door leading to the cells and returned a few minutes later.

'I was very interested,' he said, 'to hear what you told me about the Morgan gang. We've been after them for a long time. We sure would like to get our hands on them, but I reckon that as soon as they think Sinclair's in custody here, they'll make themselves scarce. They'll be expecting me to send a big posse down there after them. Trouble is, all my deputies are tied up just now.'

'I think you're right,' said Jack, 'but that isn't the end of it as far as I'm concerned. As soon as the trial's over I'm going after Morgan and his gang. They have a lot to answer for. They tortured and killed Mr Carson's cousin, they kidnapped Mr Carson and his daughter and they roughed me up considerable.'

'One man going after the Morgan gang alone sounds to me pretty much like suicide,' said Baxter.

'Two men,' said Tex.

'Let's make it three,' said Milt.

'That's better,' said Baxter, 'but still pretty dangerous.'

He pondered for a moment, then continued. 'Tell
you what,' he said. 'I'll swear you three in as deputies
to go after Morgan and his gang. If I had some
deputies to spare I'd send them with you, but I ain't.
But if you do locate the gang, don't take too many
risks. Get word to me and I'll try and send some help
along to you.

'And just in case Morgan goes into Indian
Territory,' he went on, 'I'll let the US marshal at Fort
Smith know that you might be operating in his area.'

'All right,' said Jack, 'we'll ride down to Bridger
after the trial and try to pick up the trail from there.'

As they left the marshal's office Carson told Jack
that he felt that he himself should join up with Jack
and his two friends in their search for the Morgan
gang.

'That's not a good idea,' said Jack, 'for three
reasons. You've got a wife and daughter to look after,
your cousin's widow at the store is going to need all
your help, and you've got a ranch to get running
again.'

'You're right,' said Carson, 'but I don't like the
idea of you three facing up to that gang alone.'

The trial of Sinclair took place a week later, and
the rancher was found guilty of the offences of
murder, horse-stealing and kidnapping. Judge
Trasker sentenced him to death by hanging.

By the time the trial was over Mary's ankle had healed sufficiently to allow her to walk without pain.

'I'm going to miss being carried around by you,' she told Jack, smiling.

'It's been good training,' said Jack, returning her smile, 'for that day when I carry you over the threshold of that home we're going to set up together. Assuming, that is, that the idea appeals to you.'

'I think it's an idea I could get to like pretty quickly,' said Mary.

'Right,' said Jack. 'We'll talk about it again later. Tomorrow we'll set off for Bridger.'

ELEVEN

When they reached Bridger three days later, in the evening, they stopped outside the livery stable to speak to Jake Durrell, the owner. Carson told him that Sinclair had been tried and hanged in Amarillo.

'Exactly what he deserved,' said Durrell.

'Do you know if Morgan's still around?' asked Carson.

'The Morgan gang and all the Box S hands rode off ten days ago,' Durrell replied. 'They were seen riding off down the valley, soon after the news hit town that you'd reached Amarillo with Sinclair. I rode out myself to your ranch and the Box S a couple of days ago, and they were both deserted.'

Carson spoke to Hank and Josh.

'Ride out to the ranch, boys,' he said, 'and first thing in the morning make a start on getting things shipshape again. I'll be out there as soon as I can make it.'

As the two hands left, Jack spoke to Brad and Jesse.

'I guess you'll be wanting to get back to your

ranch,' he said. 'And when you've settled in why don't you ride back to the Box S and pick up them stolen quarter horses if they're still there?'

'We'll do that,' said Brad, as he and his brother took their leave of Carson and the three deputies.

Jack and the others rode along to the store. Emily Drury and Ellen Carson were inside, in the process of closing the store for the day. Emily's face was strained as the two women greeted Carson and his daughter, and Jack. As Emily led the way into the living-room she broke down briefly, and Mary and Ellen comforted her until she recovered. Then Carson spoke.

'Emily,' he said. 'We can't begin to say how sorry we are about George. And Ellen and Mary and me, we feel responsible in a way, coming here to stay with you like we did.'

'No, no!' she said. 'Don't blame yourselves. We both wanted you to come.'

'We're all here now to help you out,' said Carson. 'If you want to carry on running the store Ellen and Mary'll help you out for a while.'

'I can't close it down,' said Emily, 'not with folks depending on it. I'll keep it running for the time being. Later, maybe I'll sell the business. I can't decide just now. Meantime, I'll sure be glad of any help I can get.'

'Morgan and his gang aren't going to get away with what they've done, Emily,' said Carson. 'Jack here and his two friends have been deputized to go after them.'

'He's an evil man,' said Emily. 'When I think of what they did to George my blood boils. I hope it ain't long before they're caught.'

Leaving the store, Jack joined Tex and Milt at the hotel and they walked along to the restaurant for a meal, while they discussed the forthcoming operation.

'Tomorrow,' said Jack, 'we'll ride over to the Box S and have a good look round, 'specially in the house. Maybe we can find some clue as to where Morgan and his gang have gone. Then we'll ride down the valley and try and pick up their trail.'

They rose early the following morning and took their leave of the Carsons and Emily Drury. Jack had a few words alone with Mary.

'Don't know how long we'll be away,' he said, 'but it's something that's got to be done. You still thinking about that proposition I put to you?'

'No need to think any more,' she smiled. 'I can't figure why, but Pa and Ma and Aunt Emily all seem to think you'd be quite a catch for an old maid like me. So I've decided I'll take a chance on you.' Then, suddenly, she was serious. 'There's something I want you to promise,' she said. 'If you catch up with Morgan and his gang and you get the chance, will you send to Marshal Baxter for help?'

'I'll do that if I can,' said Jack, 'but I can't promise there'll be enough time.'

When Jack and his companions reached the Box S ranch house they found no one inside. Likewise, the other buildings were deserted. Looking over at the pasture Jack was sure that some, if not all, of the horses stolen from the Jordan ranch were still there.

They went back into the house and looked through Sinclair's desk. There was no cash inside it and Jack guessed that Morgan had taken with him all the money he could lay his hands on. They looked at the papers in the desk but found nothing which would help them to trace Morgan.

They were just about to give up the search when Jack noticed a small drawer out of sight under the writing surface of the desk. He pulled it open and took out a sheet of paper. He examined it closely. It was a telegram, which read: 'Job accepted. Pay agreed. Must be in advance. With you in two to three days. M.' The date on which the telegram had been sent was undecipherable, but the office from which it had been transmitted was shown as 'Broken Lance'.

'I know where that is,' said Jack. 'I ain't never been there, but I've heard of it. It's in the south-west corner of Indian Territory, north of the Red River.'

'You figure that telegram's from Morgan?' asked Tex.

'Bound to be,' said Jack, putting the paper in his pocket. 'You know as well as I do that there's a lot of outlaws who hide from the law in Indian Territory. It was a stroke of luck that telegram turning up. There's a chance that Morgan and his gang have gone back into hiding somewhere near Broken Lance. I figure we should ride over there and have a good look around.'

'Seems a good idea,' said Milt, and Tex nodded in agreement.

They had just left the house and were walking towards their horses when they saw a lone rider heading towards them. They stood still, awaiting his arrival. As he drew close, something about him grabbed their attention. He was a middle-aged man, sitting uncomfortably on his horse, and he bore an uncanny resemblance to Jed Sinclair. As he pulled up in front of them he could see the 'Deputy Marshal' badges pinned to the vests of Jack and his companions.

'Howdy,' he said. 'The name's Sinclair, Ralph Sinclair. This ranch belonged to my brother. I'm his only kin.'

Curious, Jack introduced himself and his two friends.

'Don't get the idea, deputies,' said Sinclair, 'that I've got any thoughts of revenge for my brother's hanging. He got exactly what he deserved. Me and my parents broke with him long ago when we realized he just wasn't capable of leading an honest life. I'm here to get things running again. Later on I'll decide whether to stay on or sell up.

'I was too late to get to the trial,' he went on, 'so I'd be obliged if you'd tell me exactly what went on here in the valley before my brother was arrested.'

Jack briefly ran through the events ending with Jed Sinclair's downfall. Then he told Ralph Sinclair that the Jordan brothers would be coming along in the near future to collect the quarter horses which

Jed Sinclair had stolen from them.

'Right,' said Sinclair. 'When they turn up I'll know what it's all about. I can't tell you how bad I feel about having a brother who's caused so much trouble around here and who's actually killed a man just out of greed.'

'You tell the people in Bridger just what you told us,' said Jack, 'and I'm pretty sure they won't hold you responsible for what your brother did.'

Leaving Sinclair, Jack and his companions rode down the valley. When they came to the way-station on the stagecoach route, Jack left a message for Marshal Baxter in Amarillo, to go on the next coach. In it he told Baxter that the Morgan gang might be hiding out near Broken Lance in Indian Territory, and that they were heading for that locality.

Jack guessed that the Morgan gang, once out of the valley, had parted from the Box S hands before heading for Indian Territory, that vast area of 70,000 square miles between Kansas and Texas. He doubted whether, after this time, there would be any clear tracks for them to follow, and he decided that they should ride straight to Broken Lance.

They arrived there four days later, after fording the Red River at a suitable point. Before making the crossing, they removed the lawmen's badges from their vests, and decided to use fictitious names for the time being.

Broken Lance was a small town, little more than a group of buildings with one street running through the middle. Jack spotted the telegraph office ahead on the right, and they rode up to it and dismounted. Jack went inside.

There was one man in the office, a cheerful-looking man in his early twenties. His name was Parry. He smiled as Jack walked up to his desk. Making a quick judgement that Parry was the sort of man who could be trusted, Jack showed him his lawman's badge, then pocketed it again.

'I'd appreciate you keeping the fact that I'm a lawman to yourself,' he said.

'Sure,' said Parry. 'I figure that you've got a good reason. What can I do for you?'

Jack showed him the telegram. 'D'you remember sending this?' he asked.

Parry, his brow furrowed in concentration, studied the sheet of paper for a while before he answered.

'I reckon I do,' he said. 'I sent it not long ago. The reason I remember it is because I thought at the time it was a bit strange that the sender just gave one letter for his name.'

'D'you remember who handed it in?' asked Jack.

Once again Parry's brow furrowed in thought.

'It was a stranger,' he said. 'I'd never seen him before.'

Jack gave him a close description of Morgan, telling him that the man he had just described was the leader of a band of outlaws. 'Could *that* be the man?' he asked.

'Maybe,' replied Parry, 'but I can't be sure. I was busy at the time and I didn't pay him much heed.

'I thought at first,' he went on, 'when you showed me that badge, that you'd come to deal with those four outlaws that's been plaguing us for the last six weeks.'

'What outlaws?' asked Jack, sharply.

'They call themselves the Barton gang,' said Parry. 'When they rode in here they just more or less took the town over. They've all got reputations as gunfighters. They don't pay for their food, tobacco or liquor, or anything else. They just take what they want, and we've no idea when they're aiming to leave. There's nobody here to face up to them, and the US marshal's in Fort Smith, 250 miles away.

'And they've threatened to harm my wife and child,' he went on, 'if I try to get the law here by using the telegraph,'

'Where are they now?' asked Jack.

'Probably in the saloon,' replied Parry. 'You aiming to do something about them?'

'I am,' replied Jack, 'when the time's right, with the help of my friends outside.' He pointed through the window at Tex and Milt. 'But I'm still counting on you not to tell anybody that we're lawmen.'

'I won't,' said Parry. 'You can be sure of that.'

Jack thanked Parry, and rejoined Tex and Milt outside. He told them what Parry had said.

'Maybe Morgan was just passing through when he sent that telegram,' said Tex.

'Maybe so,' said Jack. 'On the other hand he and his men might be hanging out somewhere nearby. I think we'll stay around here for a few days and see if anything turns up. We'd better go get some rooms at the hotel.

'As for the Barton gang,' he went on, 'we'd better be ready for trouble from them. Whatever happens, I don't want anybody around here but Parry to know that we're lawmen. If Morgan *is* near here and he hears there are lawmen around he might move on.'

They led their horses over to the livery stable, then took rooms at the hotel next door. Leaving the others resting in their rooms, Jack went across to the barber's shop, with the intention of getting a haircut. As he crossed the road, four men who had just come out of the saloon observed him with interest. They were all tough-looking characters, and each of them was carrying a right-hand gun.

Jack saw the four, and was sure that they must be the members of the Barton gang. Tex, looking out of the window of his room, came to the same conclusion. Glancing upward at the hotel, Jack saw Tex's face at the window.

He went into the barber's shop. There were no customers inside as he sat down on the barber's chair and asked for a haircut. The barber, a small, middle-aged man, covered the upper part of Jack's body with a large cloth, and picking up a comb and a pair of scissors he started to trim Jack's hair.

The shop door opened, and two of the men who had been standing outside the saloon walked in. One of them was Barton, the leader of the gang, a burly, hard-faced man. The other was Fletcher, one of his men, smaller than the leader but just as surly-looking. The couple stood just inside the door, looking at Jack.

'You!' said Barton to Jack.

Jack raised his eyebrows, but did not speak.

'Get out of that chair,' said Barton, 'and get out of town. We don't want no gun-toting strangers here.'

'I came in here for a haircut,' said Jack, 'and that's what I aim to get. And I like the look of this town. I'm figuring to stay on here for a while, and no two-bit gunslingers are going to stop me.'

Barton's face flushed with anger. 'You just signed your own death warrant, mister,' he said, and both the outlaws went for their guns. The barber dropped down behind the barber's chair.

With his left hand Jack flung aside the cloth which the barber had placed on him, to reveal the Peacemaker in his right hand. His first shot struck Barton in the chest before the outlaw leader had triggered his gun. The second outlaw, startled by the sudden appearance of the revolver in Jack's hand, fired fractionally after Jack had triggered his gun a second time. His shot went wide, and hit in the chest by Jack's second bullet, he slumped to the floor.

Outside, there was the sound of shouting, then a brief burst of gunfire. Jack rose from the chair, ran to the window, and looked out. The barber, white-faced, peered out from behind him. Outside the shop, in the middle of the street, the two remaining outlaws were lying motionless on the ground. Tex and Milt, who was holding his left forearm, were running towards the men on the ground. A crowd was collecting.

Jack heaved a sigh of relief. Briefly, he leant over the two men on the floor, then turned to the barber.

'These two men are dead,' he said. 'Can you get the undertaker to come for them? And those two outside don't look too good either.'

The barber nodded, and, still shaking a little, ran out of the shop and along the street. Jack went outside. Tex and Milt, running towards the barber's shop, stopped as they saw him. Jack walked up to them.

'You hit, Milt?' he asked.

'Just a graze on the forearm,' replied Milt. 'It's nothing.'

'What happened out here?' asked Jack.

'We were outside the hotel,' said Tex 'and when we heard those shots from inside the barber's shop we saw these two outlaws starting to run over there. When we hollered at them to stay where they were, they turned and started shooting at us. So we fired back. They're both dead.'

Shortly after, when the undertaker had taken the four bodies away on a buckboard, Parry came out of the telegraph office as Jack and his partners were walking past it. Jack introduced him to Tex and Milt.

'You still want it keeping quiet that you're lawmen?' asked Parry.

'Yes,' said Jack,' it's important to us. And there's one other thing you could do. We'll be staying here for a while. If you happen to see that man who sent the telegram, will you let us know right away?'

'Sure,' said Parry. 'Maybe you'd like to know,' he went on, 'that the townspeople here reckon that you did them a great big favour, getting rid of the Barton gang like you did.'

Later in the day a number of townspeople thanked Jack and his partners for dealing with the Barton gang. One of them was Baldwin, the storekeeper, who told them that the gang had taken several hundred dollars' worth of goods from the store without paying. Jack suggested that any money found on the outlaws should be used to reimburse him and other business people in the town in a similar position.

'A good idea,' said Baldwin, and hurried off to see the undertaker.

Jack and his friends spent the next few days hanging around town, keeping an eye on people riding or driving in from outside. As time went by they began to get the feeling that the Morgan gang was not in the area, and eventually they decided to leave.

The question was, in which direction should they continue their search? They were discussing the possibilities over a meal in the restaurant when Jack happened to glance through the window towards the store. He saw a man loading some provisions on to a buckboard. After the first glance he turned his head away, then, realizing there was something familiar about the man, he looked again, then spoke urgently to his partners.

'That man over there near the buckboard,' he

said, pointing through the window. 'Don't he look familiar to you?'

'He sure does,' said Tex. 'He's Warner, one of Morgan's men. I heard Sinclair call him by name once.'

'This is a stroke of luck,' said Jack. 'It looks like he's getting supplies to take out to the others, wherever they are. If we follow him there's a good chance we'll find Morgan's hide-out.

'We'll keep well behind him,' he went on, 'so's he don't know he's being followed. And we'd better use our glasses to look well ahead on both sides of the trail, in case Morgan's posted a lookout to watch for riders coming in his direction.'

As they watched the man outside he finished loading the buckboard, then walked along to the saloon and disappeared inside.

'Get ready to leave,' said Jack to his partners, 'but keep out of Warner's sight. And saddle my horse for me. I'm going over to the store for a few minutes. I'll meet you behind the hotel. We can see from there when Warner leaves.'

There were no customers in the store when Jack walked in and asked the storekeeper if he knew the man in charge of the buckboard outside, and where he came from.

'Never seen him before,' said Baldwin. 'And he's pretty close-mouthed. When he left I didn't know any more about him than I did when he came in. All the same, he's the sort of customer I like to see. He pretty near filled that buckboard with supplies.'

Jack left the store and walked around to the back of it, then along the backs of the buildings lining the street until he came to the hotel. Ten minutes later Tex and Milt joined him there, leading three saddled horses. Twenty minutes later, looking along the alley between the hotel and the adjacent building, they saw Warner leave, heading east out of town.

They waited until he was well clear of town, then started to follow him, keeping well back out of sight and scanning the area ahead for any sign of a look-out.

Warner kept moving steadily until nightfall, when he stopped and lit a fire. He was obviously going to camp out for the night. During the night Jack and his partners kept watch on Warner's camp in case the outlaw moved off before dawn. But it was well after sun-up by the time he got moving again.

They followed him as they had done on the previous day. Just around noon, Jack, who was looking at the buckboard through his glasses, saw Warner bring it to a halt close to a small hill which rose from the side of the trail. Shortly after this he saw a man holding a rifle make his way down the hill to the buckboard. He stood by it for ten minutes, apparently conversing with Warner. Then the buckboard started moving again and the man who had come down the hill climbed back to the top and disappeared from view.

'So there *is* a lookout,' said Jack. 'Maybe it means we're getting close to the hide-out. What we'll do is leave the trail here and make our way around the back of that lookout point, using that low ridge we can see from here as cover. We'll come back to the trail later on, out of sight of the man who's watching it.

'But I reckon, Tex,' he went on, 'that it'd be a good idea if you followed on well behind Milt and me in case we run into trouble. It strikes me that maybe Morgan has some tricks up his sleeve for dealing with visitors who ain't welcome, and we don't want to risk all three of us being caught at the same time.'

Tex stayed where he was, while Jack and Milt took a route to the end of the ridge which Jack had recently pointed out. This route kept them out of sight of the lookout they had seen recently with Warner. They worked their way around the end of the ridge, then headed east along its south side, parallel to the trail.

What they failed to see was a rider further south who caught sight of them as he was climbing out of a ravine. The rider quickly sought cover, then dismounted and studied Jack and Milt closely through his field-glasses. Then he remounted, and keeping out of sight of Jack and Milt, he headed east at a fast pace.

When, some time later, Jack and his partner got back to the trail again, they could see from the tracks that the buckboard had passed recently. At the next bend in the trail they were able to see about a mile ahead. The buckboard was not in sight. They rode along after it, taking advantage of whatever cover there was.

As they approached the next bend in the trail, skirting a small grove of trees, they slowed down to walking pace. Suddenly, and entirely unexpectedly, five men ran out from inside the grove and surrounded them. Two of them carried shotguns, the rest handguns. Jack and Milt recognized the men, who included Warner and Rafferty, as members of Morgan's gang who had been with him when he was working for Sinclair. Morgan was not present. Jack and his partner knew that any armed resistance would almost certainly result in their immediate deaths. They sat motionless in the saddle, their hands well away from their revolvers.

On Rafferty's order one of the other men disarmed Jack and Milt, taking both their revolvers and rifles. Then the *segundo* spoke to them.

'Dunno how you two managed to follow us here,' he said, 'but it sure ain't done you no good. You were crazy to come after us. We'd finish you off right now if it weren't for the fact that we think that the boss might like to see you both die. And he's away just now. Should be back the day after tomorrow, in the morning.

'Meantime,' he went on, 'we'll hold you at the ranch, and you can think about what we're going to do to you when the boss gets back.'

The outlaws mounted their horses, which had been concealed on the far side of the grove, and two of them took the reins of the prisoners' mounts. Then they continued along the trail for about a mile and turned off it into a small basin in which four shacks had been built, two of them larger than the others. There was also a small corral and a fenced-in pasture.

Jack and Milt were put in one of the smaller shacks, at the centre of the group of buildings. They were thoroughly searched, then tied hand and foot. The search had revealed the 'Deputy Marshal' badges and Rafferty looked concerned.

'The sooner the boss gets back, the better,' he said, 'Personally, I'd like to finish these two off right now.'

TWELVE

Through his glasses Tex saw the ambush and the capture of Jack and Milt, though he could not see Morgan himself among the outlaws present. He was relieved to see that his friends had been taken without, apparently, any shots being fired.

With extreme caution he followed the outlaws and their prisoners, and from a piece of high ground well to the south of the trail he watched as Jack and Milt were taken into the small shack. As night approached he lay on the ground near the top of the slope, watching the shacks and thinking up a rescue plan.

He decided that after midnight he would sneak up to the basin and look around. It may be that he would find that a guard had been posted on the shack. If so, he would have to put him out of action before releasing his friends. It was dark now, and he decided to move closer to the buildings.

The high ground on which he had been lying was a short, flat-topped ridge which had a gentle slope on the south side up which he had ridden the previous evening. But on the north side the slope near the top was quite precipitous, dotted with an occasional stunted tree. Further down it gave way to a sheer drop of sixty feet.

Tex rose and started to walk towards his horse, which was tethered on the south slope. In the darkness he misjudged his position, came too close to the top of the north slope, and the ground crumbled beneath his feet. He lost his balance and slid down the steep slope, trying vainly to arrest his fall.

Then, suddenly, his left arm and shoulder smashed into the trunk of a small tree. Desperately he clamped his arms around it and came to a stop, his legs stretching down the slope, six feet above the sheer drop below. He felt a pain in his shoulder, but did not think that it was broken or dislocated. With an effort he brought his legs up the slope and around the trunk, then sat straddling the trunk with his arms around it.

He considered trying to climb back up the slope, but decided that it was so steep that to attempt this in the dark with an injured shoulder would be far too risky. He would have to wait until daylight came.

He spent a most uncomfortable night, holding on to the tree trunk, forcing himself not to doze off. As soon as the sun rose, acutely conscious of the fact that he was in full view of any of the outlaws who might happen to look in his direction, he started the slow difficult climb up the slope, digging the toes of his boots into the surface to obtain a purchase.

Twice his foothold crumbled away and he slid back a yard or so, fighting desperately until he managed to arrest his downward movement. But eventually he reached the top of the slope, clambered on to the flat top of the ridge, and lay on the ground for a while, recovering his strength.

His recent efforts had accentuated the pain in his left shoulder., but feeling it, he was fairly sure now that there was no fracture or dislocation. He twisted round and looked down towards the shacks below.

There were no signs of movement for the next twenty minutes. Then one man came out of a shack, saddled a horse, and rode off along the trail to the west. Shortly after, two more men came out of the same shack. Each of them was carrying something which he took into the shack in which the prisoners were being held. After a while they came out and returned to the building from which they had emerged earlier.

Throughout the day, spreadeagled against a boulder on top of the ridge, and praying that his friends were still alive, Tex kept the shacks under observation. From time to time men moved in and out of the shacks, including the one in which the prisoners had been put the previous evening, but Tex saw no sign of Morgan, a bigger man than the rest. He had observed that the six outlaws were using the two larger shacks, three of them in each.

In the afternoon, to his great relief, Tex saw Jack and Milt escorted out of the shack, to be returned a short while after. Later on, not long before nightfall, the same rider who had ridden off to the west early in the day returned.

Tex guessed that Morgan was not at present at the hide-out, which would account for the fact that Tex and his partner were still alive. He decided that he must go down after dark and release his friends.

He waited until midnight before making a move. Then he rode down the south side of the ridge, circled round, and approached the group of shacks from the west. He tied his horse to a small tree just outside the basin and continued on foot towards the shacks. The night was dark and he could barely see the outlines of the buildings. He halted and looked in the direction of the shack in which his friends were imprisoned. Briefly a match flared outside it and he could see the glowing end of a cigarette.

Moving silently in the dark, Tex circled around inside the basin and came up behind the guarded shack. Creeping around the side of it, he peered around the corner and saw the outline of the guard. He was standing halfway along the front wall, outside the door. This man, thought Tex, must be put out of action without alerting the other members of the gang.

He stepped around the corner, holding his double-edged Bowie knife by the blade, and coughed. Startled, the guard swung round, reaching for his six-shooter. With unerring accuracy Tex threw the knife, the long sharp blade lodging in the guard's chest. The victim gave a strangled shout, then collapsed on the ground. He had not fired.

Tex walked up to his victim, retrieved his knife and took the two guns that the man was wearing. As he had expected, the guard was dead. He waited for a short while to see whether the man's shout had been heard, but all was quiet. He slid back the heavy bolt on the door of the shack, walked inside, and pulled the door to behind him.

'It's Tex,' he called out quietly as he lit a match. By its light he could see his two friends lying on the floor with their hands and legs bound. He extinguished the flame and knelt down beside the two prisoners. He felt for the ropes around their wrists and ankles and severed them with the keen blade of his Bowie. Then he placed a revolver in Jack's hand and another in Milt's.

'These are from the dead guard outside,' he said. 'Looks like he fancied himself as a gunfighter.'

'We're sure glad to see you,' said Jack. 'When you didn't turn up last night, we figured you were in trouble.'

'I was,' said Tex. 'Tell you about it later. What's our next move?'

'How many men are there here tonight?' asked Jack, guessing that Tex had been watching the buildings all day.

'Six, counting the dead guard,' replied Tex. 'They're living in the two bigger shacks, three men in each.'

'We'll take the five outlaws prisoner then,' said Jack. 'This is as good a time as any.'

They left the shack and stood for a moment looking towards the two larger shacks.

'We'll go in them one at a time,' said Jack. 'The

one on the left first. And when we go in there we must keep the noise down if we can, so's the men in the second one don't hear us.'

He went back into the shack they had just left and came out carrying an oil lamp.

'I'll light this just before we go in,' he said.

Quietly, they approached their objective, and paused outside while Jack lit the lamp and opened the door. They moved quickly inside as Jack placed the lamp on a table. They could see three men sleeping on mattresses on the floor. Each of them was rudely awakened by the muzzle of a six-gun jammed against the side of his neck and their weapons were thrown aside. They were told that the slightest noise from them would result in a bullet through the head. Then, quickly, their hands were bound and they were gagged.

Leaving Milt to watch the three outlaws, Tex and Jack, using a lamp which was hanging on the wall, walked over to the second shack and repeated the exercise, capturing the two outlaws inside without any problems arising. They escorted them over to join the other three prisoners.

Jack and Tex went to look at the other small shack, to find that it was being used as a makeshift cook-shack, equipped with a stove and a chimney through the roof. Inside, in a cupboard, they found the weapons and badges which had been taken from them earlier.

'We know that Morgan's due back this morning,' said Jack, 'so we've got to be ready for him. We'll bring

all his men in here and tie them up and gag them.
We'll keep the stove going and make plenty of smoke,
so's he'll think his men are in here when he turns up.
But *we'll* be inside as well, ready to take him. He's sure
going to get a surprise when he opens that door.

'There's just one possible snag,' Jack went on. 'If
Morgan rides in along the main trail from the west,
maybe he'll wonder why his lookout is missing. It's a
risk we'll have to take.'

Tex took his own horse and those of his partners
and tethered them out of sight in a small patch of
brush outside the basin. Meanwhile, Jack and Milt
escorted all five outlaws into the cookshack and
forced them to lie, bound and gagged, on the floor.
Then they dragged the body of the dead outlaw into
a patch of brush well away from the buildings. After
that, they waited for daylight to come.

When it arrived, they ate some food, keeping
watch through the cookshack window over the
entrance to the basin, and settled down to await
Morgan's arrival. From time to time they put more
wood on the stove. Just before eleven o'clock, Milt, at
the window, called out.

'It's him,' he said, 'riding in from the east.'

'Then he don't know there's a missing lookout,'
said Jack. 'That's good.'

They watched as Morgan rode up to the shack
where two of the outlaws had been captured,
dismounted and walked inside.

'When I give the word,' said Jack, 'the three of
us'll start laughing as loud as we can.'

Morgan emerged shortly after and looked over at the cookshack. He saw the smoke belching from the chimney and heard a burst of laughter coming through the open window from inside. He started walking in that direction.

When he reached the shack he pushed the door open and started to enter, to be brought up sharply by the muzzle of Jack's gun pressed against his side. Tex relieved the outlaw of his gun. Morgan tried to grab Tex's gun from the holster, but Jack rapped him hard over the head with the barrel of his Peacemaker and the outlaw, temporarily stunned, slumped to the floor. In a trice he was tied up and laid on the floor against his men.

'Well,' said Jack, with grim satisfaction. 'It looks like this is the end of the trail. Let's bury the dead one, then we can take these prisoners to Broken Lance. Maybe we can get some lawmen from Fort Smith to take them off our hands.'

Milt hitched a couple of horses to the buckboard and drove it over to the cookshack. Then they dragged the six prisoners out and lifted them on to the buckboard.

'A tight fit,' commented Jack, 'but that don't bother me none.'

Their arrival in Broken Lance caused a minor sensation. A growing crowd accompanied the buckboard as Jack drove it up to the telegraph office and stopped outside. Parry came out to see what all the excitement was about. He stared at the six prisoners on the buckboard.

'You found the Morgan gang?' he asked.

Jack nodded. 'I want to let Fort Smith know,' he said.

'Maybe you don't need to,' said Parry. 'There's a couple of US deputy marshals from Fort Smith, called Lord and Harker, in town right now. In fact, I can see them heading this way.'

He pointed to two men wearing lawmen's badges who were approaching.

The men walked up to the buckboard and examined the contents with interest. Then Lord, the older of the two, turned to Jack and his partners.

'One of you Jack Silver?' he asked.

Jack nodded and introduced his friends.

'We had word from Amarillo,' said Lord, 'that you were down here chasing the Morgan gang. You done a good job. We'll take them off your hands and get a jail wagon here as soon as we can.'

'That suits us fine,' said Jack. 'We'll head back for Amarillo and hand in our badges.'

One week later Mary Carson, concerned. by Jack's continuing absence, was driving the buckboard back from Bridger to the Carson ranch when she heard two distant gunshots behind her. Looking back, she saw a rider racing towards her, and as he drew closer she thought she recognized the big chestnut. Seconds later she was sure of it. She breathed a huge sigh of relief as she reined in the horses, and the buckboard came to a halt.

Jack brought his mount to a sliding stop beside

her, jumped down, and tied his horse to the buck-board.

'You still figure you can put up with me for a husband?' he asked.

'I'm sure of it,' she replied. 'And don't you ever leave me like that again, Jack Silver.'

'There's no chance of that,' said Jack. He climbed on to the seat beside her, gave her a kiss, and took over the reins.